About the Author

Robert Heath hitchhiked from Yorkshire to Morocco to take up his first teaching post at the American School of Tangier in 1978. Since then, he has criss-crossed the globe, teaching PE and coaching football in over a dozen International Schools on four continents.

Dedication

To Felicity, with heartfelt thanks for your
encouragement and support.

Rob Heath

A TANGERINE DREAM

AUSTIN MACAULEY
PUBLISHERS LTD.

A CIP catalogue record for this title is available from the British Library.

ISBN 9781786292568 (Paperback)
ISBN 9781786292575 (Hardback)
ISBN 9781786292582 (eBook)
www.austinmacauley.com

First Published (2017)
Austin Macauley Publishers Ltd.
25 Canada Square
Canary Wharf
London
E14 5LQ

Pushmepullyou gear levers

Somewhere around one a.m., I was woken from my slumber by the sound of a rather furtive knocking at my door. Peeking through the spyhole, I saw two dark faces, one of which I recognised. It was Abdelhamid El Habsi, a student at the American School of Tangier, where I was employed as a PE teacher.

I opened the door.

"It won't start," said El Habsi, in a slightly frantic whisper which was just a couple of notches lower than a shout.

"Well, you'll have to push it then."

"Yeah. We tried that, but the hill's too steep."

He paused. There was a short but definite pause, during which time I divined what he really wanted.

"Do you want me to help you?" I asked, hardly believing what I was saying, but at the same time realising that there was no other feasible option.

"Er, yes," El Habsi said, rather sheepishly.

Which is how I came to find myself helping one of my own students and his friend steal my own car. I bunged on a pair of shorts and a t-shirt, and ran down the stairs with the two youths. The car was sitting at the foot of the ramp leading up out of the carpark. The night was very quiet, and there didn't seem to be anyone watching from any of the windows of the apartment buildings which surrounded us. We all applied our shoulders to the rear, and we were soon at the top. El Habsi jumped into the driving seat, and without any further exchanges, I headed back to my apartment. As I walked back down the ramp, I heard the car spluttering to life as it coasted down the steep hill towards the beach. I breathed a sigh of relief.

The car in question was a beige Citroen 2CV, with British licence plates. It had been in my possession for slightly less than a week.

Quite late on the previous Saturday, I had found myself seated at a bar in Tangier, next to a young American. We struck up a conversation, during the course of which he mentioned that he was trying desperately to sell his car. He had bought it somewhere in Europe three months ago, had driven it all over the continent and down into Morocco, and now needed to unload it before flying back to the States. He only wanted two hundred dollars for it, but there was one problem; it had no papers. There was nothing to prove ownership, no insurance, nothing.

With the enthusiasm that often gets the better of young men in bars late on Saturday nights, I thought to myself that this sounded like the deal of a lifetime. I didn't imagine that the lack of papers would be a major problem in a city like Tangier, and I didn't think that the lack of any dollars at all in my possession was an altogether insurmountable problem either. So I pledged to buy it, and he agreed to bring it to the same bar the following evening.

Soon after waking the next morning, I remembered. "Hmmm," I thought. "Two hundred dollars. How can I get hold of two hundred dollars by tonight?" Even in the cold, grey light of dawn (actually it was a beautifully clear and crisp sunny morning, but anyway...), I felt like I should be able to figure out a way of finding that sum by nightfall. After all, I was in Tangier.

Tangier in those days was a remarkable city. It didn't quite possess the romance and intrigue of Bogart's and Bergman's *Casablanca*, but it came close; a lot closer than the real Casablanca, incidentally. Even in my few months' residence there, I had met some extraordinary characters, and heard tell of myriads more. There were the millionaires, swanning it in their superlative villas up on 'the mountain' overlooking the city. There were the sexual refugees – mostly men of a certain bent, shall we say, fleeing the narrow-minded and repressive societies of Europe and the USA for the free-and-easy attitudes (not to mention the equally easy, if not quite free, availability of delicious and amenable young brown bottoms) of Morocco. There were various other refugees as well. I knew a man who was a convicted murderer, released from a Scottish prison after serving twenty-seven years of a life sentence, General Franco's sister, a White Russian princess and an ex-professional goaltender for the Boston Bruins. Indeed, there was an atmosphere, and an unspoken assumption, amongst the foreigners in the city that everyone had some reason, overt or not, but almost always 'ulterior', for living in Tangier rather than where they came from.

9

And that was just the foreigners. Of course, the city was mostly peopled by Moroccans, but they themselves were an extraordinary lot. Many true Tangerines were urbane and cosmopolitan. Almost everybody spoke three languages (Moroccan Arabic, French and Spanish). They were relaxed and tolerant Muslims, happily accepting, nay even embracing, alcohol, hashish and sex. But there were also many Moroccans in the city who had emigrated from much more traditional rural areas far away. Farmers from the interior come north to sell their produce, Berbers from the Atlas Mountains, jet black tribesmen from the deep south.

Tangier was also, of course, a major international port. So on top of all the richness of the various resident groups, you could add the flavour and intrigue associated with sailors and goods from all over the world flowing in and out of the city, some of which were perfectly legal, but others less so. From the window of my apartment, I could watch the port, and on any given day, queuing up to get inside the harbour walls along with the luxury cruise liners, the container vessels and the ferries from Gibraltar and Algeciras, I could see terrible old rustbuckets flying Panamanian or Liberian flags, and you had to wonder precisely what their business was.

The final layer on the unique urban cake that was Tangier was composed of the tourists. The city was a major destination for Europeans looking for the magic combination of beach, food and nightlife. For the nine months of the year when the weather was good, Tangier was full of lobster-coloured, scantily-clad groups walking the streets, followed invariably by two or three touts offering them any and every service imaginable (and some that were not imaginable). Of course, there are places all over the world where tourists get hassled by the locals. But I doubt whether there is anywhere, with the possible exception of Marrakesh, where the indigenous population are as aggressively persistent and annoying as Tangier. The standard exchange between hassler and victim usually began with smiles and exaggerated politeness on both sides, went through a more frosty phase where the foreigners tried first of all rudeness and then simply ignoring their adversary, and terminated in a verbally and often physically violent confrontation, as often as not including mutual death threats.

Anyway, on that Sunday morning, that was the city I ventured forth into in search of two hundred dollars. I went first of all to the Café des Sports on the main Rue Pasteur, just round the corner from my apartment. Over a café au lait and croissant, I considered my options. Could I borrow the money from one of my teaching colleagues at AST? No, was the very quick answer I gave myself to that question. The salaries at that school were woeful, and my friends were all in the same boat as me – i.e. we were into the third week of the month, so we were already living on credit until the next payday. Was there anything I could sell? No, not really, except, it being Tangier, probably my body, and what I would have to do to earn two hundred dollars I did not even want to think about, except to say that I didn't want that car that badly. Crime? No. Again, I didn't want the car enough to risk the horrors of a Moroccan jail. Not to mention the fact that I was totally inexperienced in criminal ways, and was unlikely to be able to plan and carry out any brilliant heist within the space of ten hours.

I ordered another coffee. Tangier was, as mentioned earlier, crawling with millionaires. Two hundred dollars would be peanuts to them. Trouble was, none of them knew me from Mohamed, and none of them were likely to let me have even two hundred peanuts. But there must be somebody I knew who had a little bit of money. After all, two hundred dollars was not a fortune, even in those days.

And then it hit me. Teresa Connor! She was perfect.

Teresa was a single woman who worked in a rather lowly position (but high enough to earn at least a reasonable salary) at the British Consulate. I had met her a few months earlier when I had joined a recreational Tuesday evening badminton group. She was a pretty sad and lonely individual, who almost certainly had nothing much better to do with her money than lend it to me. She was also from Shipley, and since I was from Leeds, we had a Yorkshirefolk-abroad bond, which I could probably exploit.

A ten minute walk took me to Teresa's apartment block, and I was lucky enough to find her in. After a few minutes of idle chatter, I brought up the subject of the car. It was beautifully done, actually. On the walk to her apartment, I had devised a cunning way of presenting her with the deal, and it wasn't long before she had agreed to go halves with me on the Bargain of the Century. We would each pay a hundred dollars and share the car. She would have it during the week (mostly, unless I wanted it), and I would have it at the weekends (unless she wanted it). And since I was a little short of readies at that particular moment, she would pay my half for me up front, and I would pay her back as soon as I was paid. I didn't bother mentioning the minor matter of the paperwork (lack thereof).

So, soon enough, I was strolling back home with the loot. She hadn't had any dollars in her apartment, but from somewhere, she fished out some sterling, and after a quick consultation of a week-old *Daily Telegraph*, we worked out that 125 quid would be just about right.

In the bar that night, the American guy duly appeared, and was perfectly happy to accept my cash. He led me outside, handed me over the keys, and with a bit of a lurch (tricky things, you know, those old 2CVs, with their pushmepullyou gear levers) I roared off into the night. When I got the car home and had a chance to examine it more closely, I found to my delight that for my 125 quid, I had acquired not only the car, but also a splendid green Moroccan blanket and a Michelin map of Morocco. This latter was a particularly valuable item, because it was unavailable, indeed banned, in the country because the government objected to where the Michelin people had marked the border with Mauretania. (Failing to take into account that Morocco had marched 200,000 people over the border a few years back and annexed a huge chunk of empty desert.)

The following morning, I very proudly drove myself to school. Technically, it being 'the week' rather than 'the weekend', Teresa should have had the car, but I felt that as a reward for my entrepreneurial endeavours I should have the thing for a couple of weeks or so. I was very disappointed that none of my colleagues actually saw me drive into school.

However, it was not long after that someone came into the staff room and asked, "Whose is that Citroen out there?"

"Oh, it's mine," I answered casually.

All eyes immediately swivelled to stare at me in what I took to be impressed amazement. After all, young newbug teachers fresh out of England did not normally acquire the status of car-owner within a few months of arrival at that school. Not on those salaries.

Feeling that an explanation was expected of me, I gave the assembled throng a brief rundown on how I had stumbled on it. My audience were gratifyingly impressed. Finally, I mentioned the absence of documentation, and asked if anyone had any ideas where I could get some papers 'made up'.

There was a bit of a silence at that. Somehow the 'hey-that-Rob-is-quite-a-guy' atmosphere I had been enjoying seemed to suddenly dissipate.

Finally, one of the older-timers said, "Are you mad? Don't you know that illegal or forged car documents are the one thing the police in this country are red-hot about?"

This was obviously a wind-up.

"Ha-ha," I said.

"No, seriously," chipped in another Smart Alec. "It's a perk that the police are allowed to keep any foreign car they confiscate."

"Yeah. Actually, they are the only Moroccans who are allowed to own a car with foreign plates. If you see any Moroccan driving around in a foreign car, you can bet that it's a policeman."

"Most of them can't afford to buy one, though, so they try to bust someone with dodgy papers. The law is two years in jail for the driver, and the car goes straight to the copper."

"I wouldn't drive that thing around if I were you."

"Right," I said. "Okay. Anyway, I've got a class now, so I'd better run."

And feeling slightly deflated, I left the staff room and headed for the PE office. On the way, I decided that things couldn't be as bad as these blokes had made out, but to be on the safe side, I would leave the car at home until I had definitively sussed the situation re car papers.

When I got to my office, I found that most of the kids in my class were already out on the court. I conducted most of my PE classes on an open air multipurpose court which was surrounded on three sides by two stories of classrooms. This particular seventh and eighth grade class was one in which I had had a few problems with the boys not allowing the girls to have a fair crack at things. So, being already in a rather tetchy mood, I was particularly miffed to see that all the boys in the class were shooting around with the few balls which I had left out there (sadly, AST was not the kind of school where you got one ball per kid), whilst all the girls were sitting on a bench. I knew for certain that the boys would have grabbed any balls off the girls and not let them use them.

Which is why I proceeded to shout at the top of my voice to the boy who I knew would have been the most likely aggressor in such a case. "Younes! Can you tell me why all you boys have got balls, and none of the girls have any?"

Staff room conversation that lunchtime was about equally divided between two topics: Younes's putative response to my question, which every teacher in the school had heard (If not the original version, they had heard it repeated a dozen times by helpful colleagues.), and the chances of me getting home in my car without being arrested.

I had driven in to school that morning with an air of jaunty optimism, but it was a much more wary and chastened driver who lurched (it takes time to get used to the 2CV's gear lever, you know) out of the school gate at three p.m. Whilst I was yet to be fully convinced about all this policeman-foreign car rigmarole, I have to admit that I was thinking that it would be a good idea not to get involved in any traffic accident or infraction which might draw me to the attention of a policeman.

It was a hot and slow crawl through the traffic down into the centre of town. My route home took me along the main thoroughfare, Rue Pasteur, from which I had to turn left, across the oncoming traffic, down the hill towards the port and my apartment. As I approached that left turn, I quite correctly moved out into the middle of the road, indicating my intention to turn. A light further down the hill had just turned green, and because a long line of cars was coming towards me, I could not make the turn straight away. So I pushed the gear lever into neutral, and yanked on the handbrake. After half a minute or so, the light changed back to red, and the stream of cars coming up the hill stopped, enabling me to make my turn. But I found that I could not release the handbrake.

As anyone who has driven a 2CV will know, the handbrake on these infernal machines consists of a ratcheted metal rod which the driver pulls out of a plastic sheath. In my nervous state, I had yanked the thing out too vigorously, pulling the last ratchet out of the casing, with the result that no matter how much I twisted the handle, the brake would not release.

Although I had pulled into the middle of the road, there was still not enough room for cars to pass inside me. I was, therefore, blocking the main street of the city. In the middle of the rush hour. Within nanoseconds of me failing to turn left when the opportunity arose, a cacophony of horns trumpeted their disapproval of my stationary condition.

As I wrestled frantically with the stupid handbrake, I heard, amongst the honking, a loud whistle blast. Looking in my mirror, I saw a very large policeman, who had been controlling the traffic further up the street, approaching the car. He looked very hot, and extremely bothered about something, and I had an inkling that he was not happy about the fact that my car was holding up all the traffic.

This was a nasty moment.

Still grappling desperately with the recalcitrant brake, I watched the policeman get closer and closer. His whistle, which he persisted in blowing, got more and more indignant, and his face got redder and redder. Visions of life in a Moroccan jail flashed before my eyes. The heat, the dark, the cockroaches, the sodomy. By the time he reached the car, and leaned his flushed face into the window, I was resigned to my fate.

"It's a fair cop," I almost said.

The cop, who was not in any way fair, shouted furiously at me in Arabic. I didn't catch much of what he said, but being a natural at languages, I deduced that it was something along the lines of "Excuse me, sir, but this vehicle is causing an obstruction of the traffic. Will you please move along sharpish."

I gestured feebly at the handbrake, and gave what I took to be an expressive shrug.

The horn blaring got louder.

The policeman shouted at me again. Then he blew his whistle at me.

In a moment of inspiration – quite impressive I thought considering the highly pressurised circumstances – I remembered the French word for brake. "La freine!" I said, repeating the eloquent shrug.

The policeman gave me a final withering look, and then shouted across to a crowded pavement café. Immediately, a dozen or so men leapt up from the tables, from where they had been hugely enjoying the spectacle of the foreigner blocking the traffic and the fat policeman getting angry, and marched out into the road, quickly surrounding the car. For one horrible moment, I thought that I was about to be dragged from the vehicle and lynched by a seething mob of hysterical Arabs. But no. On a word from the policeman, the men all took a grip of the underside of the car, and bodily bounced the thing across the road!

This surprising intervention solved the immediate problem; the traffic was now once more free to crawl out of the city. But I now expected the real trouble to begin. The policeman was now also free to ask me for my papers, and surely the game was up. I had been sitting in a motionless car in the full afternoon sun for several minutes now, grappling with the handbrake and facing the stress of imminent arrest. Utterly drained, I sat meekly at the wheel, awaiting the inevitable.

But after a pause, it dawned on me that the policeman had not returned to berate me as expected. I looked around and saw that he was still standing in the middle of the road, supervising the returning traffic flow. A thought occurred to me, and I grabbed the handbrake again. It released! The bouncing of the car must have shaken it free.

Without a backward glance, I roared off down the sidestreet. I still expected to hear the policeman whistling at me to stop as he was still planning to deal with me when he got a moment, but no whistle came. In a few minutes I had the car parked and was slumped exhausted in the cool safety of my apartment.

I decided I would not use the car again until I had either got some papers for it, or had found out for sure what the story was re these bloody policemen. For the next couple of days, the car sat in the carpark while I made absolutely no progress with my research into those two questions. Nobody I asked, either at school or in The Nautilus bar, where I was occasionally known to hang out, had any idea how I could 'acquire' a set of car papers. Everybody seemed to agree, however, that avaricious Moroccan policemen would undoubtedly be circling my car like sharks around the wreckage of a sinking ship.

Quite late on the Thursday evening, I was sitting reading in my apartment when there came a knock on my door. Peeking through the eyehole, I saw to my horror a man standing there. The horror came not from the fact that he was a man, but from the fact that he was wearing a uniform.

Surely this was it. They had somehow found out who owned the car, and had come now to demand the papers. My carefree life was over, my nascent career in ruins, and all I could look forward to was gruel and buggery. I contemplated briefly just not opening the door, but I reasoned that he had probably heard me shuffling about already, and so a failure to open up would look suspicious.

So, with dread flooding through me, I slowly opened the door. I almost presented my wrists for the handcuffs, and said "Okay, lead me away." But there was still a small hope somewhere in my soul that perhaps this policeman was here for some other, perfectly innocent and non-going-to-jail reason. Making a collection for the Tangier Police Widows' Fund, for example.

"Bonsoir," I said.

"Bonsoir, monsieur. Excusez-moi. Does that Citroen with the English plates down in the car park belong to you?"

Wild thoughts now flashed into my panic-stricken brain. The game's up! Okay, I'll admit the whole thing, just don't beat me! Deny it! There's nothing to tie me to that car. But what if they have witnesses who've seen me drive it? Or fingerprints? What if he knows the car's mine but doesn't know there is anything illegal about it? If I deny it, his suspicions will be aroused.

I opened my mouth to reply, still not knowing whether I was going to say yes, no or kind of. Eventually, a 'oui' emerged, sounding, I hoped non-committal enough that I could later retract it if necessary.

"Because I was wondering if you would be interested in selling it."

Selling it? Hey-hey! He hadn't come to arrest me! He just wanted to buy the car. Relief coursed through my body. Suddenly, I even saw a way out of this impasse. I could sell the car to this copper, get it off my hands, stay out of jail, and maybe even make a profit.

"Em, well, maybe..." I answered.

"Bien, because I saw it parked down there and asked around about who it belonged to. I live in the opposite building. As a policeman, I am allowed to own a car with foreign plates, so I thought that if you wanted to sell..."

While he was rambling on, it occurred to me with horror (again) that of course I couldn't sell the thing to this policeman, because he would need to see the documents.

"Well," I said, "I don't think I actually want to sell it just now."

He looked disappointed.

"But if I do, I will definitely give you first refusal."

"Très bien. Here is my card."

After assuring him several more times that I would go to him straight away if I did indeed ever decide to sell the car, he finally left.

That was when I decided that I was going to have to lose this damned car, and thinking about how best to achieve that aim, my mind alighted on El Habsi.

Although nominally an eleventh grade student at AST, Abdelhamid El Habsi was really more of an entrepreneur and general wide boy. He was reputed to be repeating eleventh grade for the fifth or sixth time, and he certainly appeared to be well into his twenties. His inability to pass eleventh grade was partly due to the fact that he rarely turned up for any classes, and even more rarely, in fact never, did any of the work which the classes required. It was also partly due to the fact that he and his father were well aware that if and when El Habsi finally graduated, he would then have to serve his compulsory two years in the army.

El Habsi's average day consisted of him swanning in to school sometime about mid-morning, hanging out in the corridors most of the day (occasionally dropping in on a class if some contact he needed for his latest deal happened to be in there), then, if he wasn't too tired or he didn't have to roar off on his motorbike on business, joining my school football team for training in the afternoon. He wasn't a bad player, either; a striker who, while not naturally gifted, had the priceless knack of scoring goals.

Apart from the fact that he was a wheeler-dealer extraordinaire, El Habsi was a particularly good candidate for getting rid of my car because I believed that his father owned a garage.

So as soon as I was free the next morning, I set off through the school corridors in search of him. I eventually tracked him down in, of all places, a History class. He was sitting near the front, paying no attention to the teacher's erudite words on the American Civil War, apparently working out some complicated mathematical problem in a small notebook. Doing his accounts, probably.

Waiting for him as he came out of the classroom, I beckoned him over to a quiet spot.

"El Habsi, is it right that your father owns a garage?"

"Yes, he does."

"Okay. Well, I've got a fantastic offer for him." I took the keys of the Citroen millstone from my pocket. "These are the keys to a Citroen 2CV. The car kind of belongs to me, but I don't want it anymore. I'll tell you where it's parked, and you can drive it away, and it's yours."

El Habsi looked at me for a few seconds. He didn't say anything, but I could see that he was not used to being offered something for nothing, and he was trying to figure out the catch.

"There's one catch," I said, to put him out of his misery.

As I anticipated, El Habsi did not seem in the least bit put out by the lack of papers. I was sure that he or his father would know how to get the necessary documents forged. He cheerfully agreed to make sure the car was gone by the next morning.

As indeed it was, although it needed a bit of a push.

I was extremely relieved to see the back of it. For the next several weeks, I was anticipating my uniformed neighbour reappearing, indignantly demanding to know why I hadn't offered him the car. My plan was to tell him the 'truth', i.e. that it had been stolen. But fortunately, I never saw him again.

There was also the small matter of the money I owed to Teresa. And the fact that she was expecting to use the car every week.

After several weeks not going to badminton, and generally avoiding the woman (desperately ducking down sidestreets when I saw her, for example), she finally cornered me at a party.

I was hoping that perhaps she had forgotten about the whole episode.

"So when am I going to see that car I paid for, not to mention the sixty-five pounds you owe me?" she said straight away, immediately disabusing me of that misconception.

I had been planning this for ages, but I still wasn't sure I could pull it off. Still, after a deep breath, I took the plunge.

"Car?"

"Yes. A Citroen, if I remember correctly."

"Teresa, you must have misunderstood me. I told you I was buying deux chevaux, right?"

"A Citroen Deux-Chevaux, that's right."

"Oh! Ha ha! Did you think I was referring to a car? Oh, I see now... a Citroen Deux-Chevaux! What a hilarious misunderstanding."

She was giving me a very cool glare, but I had no choice but to blunder on.

"No, what I meant was that I was buying shares in two racehorses."

"But... but... what was all that about me driving at the week and you during the weekend?"

"I don't remember that, Teresa. Anyway, don't worry. As soon as one of these nags wins a race, I'll pass over your share of the winnings."

She still looked extremely doubtful.

"So what are these horses called?" she asked, suspiciously.

"Oh, er... Gullible and, erm... Taken For A Ride. I think Gullible is running at Kempton Park this week. Anyway, gotta dash!"

And the whole episode was not a complete oil spill; I still had the blanket and the (illegal) Michelin map of Morocco.

Callisthenics

The first, innocuous link in the miraculous chain of events which led me to Morocco had been forged during the previous Christmas holiday.

I had finished a three-year degree course in Geography at Leeds University a couple of years earlier. My main priority during that time was to play as much football as I could.

Every Wednesday and Saturday I would be playing for one of the university teams (mostly the Second XI, but I did have a good run one year in the Firsts) up at the Weetwood sports fields or at venues scattered across the north of England. Such a programme should have been feasible, even with training thrown in a couple of nights a week, in conjunction with a reasonable amount of studying geography. What really held me back were the indoor leagues in the sports hall.

They had leagues organised all throughout the day, every day of the week. You could get a group of blokes together who were free at, say, ten on Tuesday mornings, and enter a team in that league. I played officially in two of these leagues. But I twigged on quite early in the piece that very often teams in these leagues had a hard time getting all their players to turn up every week. This meant that if someone (me, for example) turned up and mooched around the gym, there was always a good chance that a team would be a player short and I (for example) could get a game.

Once I had made this discovery, I took to bringing a bag with my kit in it into university every day, just in case the opportunity should arise for me to saunter over to the sports hall on the off chance. This then led me to the recurrent dilemma as I sat over my daily coffee in the Student Union: should I go to the Geog. Dept. and sit through a riveting two hour lecture on soil profiles in north Wales and their historical significance, or should I slide over to the sports hall and see if I could pick up a game?

I didn't get a very good degree.

This caused me a lot of grief, because I really wanted to stay on in Leeds and continue not going to lectures and playing football instead. Unfortunately, the only continuing course that would accept me was in Education. So I managed to persuade my parents to contribute to my grant for a one-year course in the teaching of Geography and PE.

When I went home at Christmas, my bankrollers were understandably anxious as to whether their investment in my teaching career was liable to bear any dividends. I felt too guilty to tell them the truth, that I had absolutely no intention of ever actually becoming a teacher and that I was only doing the course as a *raison d'être a Leeds.* So I dreamed up a condition which I thought was a foolproof way of ensuring that I would not actually have to get a teaching job. I declared that I was only interested in PE jobs overseas. Since my course only contained a vague smattering of PE content, and since I figured there was no chance that any plum schools in exotic locations would be remotely interested in me, I was convinced that this stipulation would leave me safe.

The morning after I explained my doctrine of employment, my mother looked up from the pages of *The Observer* and said, "Here's a job for you, Rob. The American School of Tangier is seeking an Athletic Director."

After listening to me enumerate a good half dozen reasons why my applying for such a job would be futile, she said, "Well, it wouldn't do any harm to just write to them, would it?"

I couldn't argue with that, given that they were forking out for my grant, so I grudgingly sat down and applied pen to paper.

As soon as I got back to Leeds after the vacation, I had to start a whole term of teaching practice. I had been placed in a private, fee-paying school in Wakefield. This should have been a breeze compared to some of the scrofulous comprehensives in places like Rotherham and Dewsbury where some of my cohorts got sent, but even so, I hated it.

I had to get up at a thoroughly unfeasible time and then try to coax my aged Ford Anglia to sputter into life. Each day I tried a wider and less successful detour than the previous one in an attempt to avoid the traffic jams, invariably arriving late and scurrying into the morning prayers under a hail of glowering scowls from the established teachers. I had to teach almost entirely

Geography, and when I was allowed to do PE I was given the challenge of motivating the gumby set to do cross-country or rugby in sleet and a freezing gale.

So when a letter arrived inviting me for an interview with the American School of Tangier at the Oxford & Cambridge Club in London on a Wednesday in February, my immediate reaction was, "Two days off TP? I'm going!"

After a slight but highly enjoyable lie in, I set off down the M1 in the Anglia, smugly eschewing the Wakefield turn off and setting my course for the deep south. I arrived without mishap (which was not always the case with that car), and spent the night near Stamford Bridge with my former Leeds University football chum Mike Neary. The following morning, I again woke up luxuriously late before getting the tube into town and sauntering along The Mall in search of the club.

I found the place ten minutes before my appointment, and went for another little walk around the block, thinking that I might be well employed considering what I might want to say. But I couldn't think of anything, and soon enough the time was up and I found myself being ushered in to a very plush lounge where I shook hands with Garfield McAllister the Third.

Mr McAllister the Third was VERY American. I can't really remember what we talked about, but I do recall that I had enough nous to make a big deal of having played for the Leeds University team which won the Northern Universities League a couple of years back. I could tell that he was impressed, and he obviously did not realise that university sports in England are not quite the big deal that they are in the States. I suppose I should have enlightened him on that point, but I couldn't quite find the appropriate moment in our conversation to do so.

The worst moment was when he asked me if I would include calisthenics in my lessons. I didn't know what callisthenics were, but of course my instinct was to just bluff my way through and say, "Why yes, of course." But what if this was the trick question he used to sort out the wheat from the chaff? So I mumbled something non-committal, and Mr McAllister the Third, who was a big and extremely imposing man, gave me a very penetrating look which seemed to say, 'You are a complete charlatan, aren't you?'

I was convinced I had failed the interview at that point, and since I had a subtext for this whole trip to London (other than getting two days off) and I needed to be getting along, I tried to expedite the whole business asap after that.

I rushed back to Chelsea, jumped in the Anglia, and roared off back up the M1 at 85 mph, which was really thrashing it in that thing. Leeds United were playing the second leg of a League Cup semi-final at Nottingham Forest that night at 7.30 p.m., and I was hoping to be there to see if my heroes could overturn the 3-1 deficit from the first leg.

I didn't hit the Nottingham turn-off until 7.20 p.m., but incredibly I breezed all the way to the ground with no holdups and found a place to leave the car close to the stadium. It was just on 7.30 p.m. as I ran up to the turnstiles to be told that the ground was full. But some lads around me had heard a rumour that they were still letting people in round the other side, so we all sprinted round the outside and came to a tiny door with a small knot of people in front of it. I joined that knot, and soon found myself squeezed through and in the ground without even paying! I ran up some steps and discovered that I was in the corner of a huge stand. There weren't any seats left, so I just sat on the steps and settled down to watch the game.

Almost immediately, Leeds were given a free kick in the middle of the park out on the left, and while a couple of players were standing near the ball preparing to knock a long ball into the box, Frank Gray came steaming up from left back and hit an absolute rocket which screamed into the top corner of the net. That put us at 2-3 and right back in it. Buoyed by such a great goal, we took total control.

On the stroke of half-time, the incomparable Tony Currie picked up the ball out near the left touchline. Currie had an amazing ability to just lazily drift away from defenders, almost by hypnosis it seemed, and he now produced one of his trademark Currie Shuffles to leave two Forest players staring at thin air while he moved infield. He then let rip with a stupendous shot from miles out which hit the corner of bar and post so hard that I swear the whole goal shook and I thought for a second it was going to collapse.

If that had gone in... But it didn't, and they scored two in the second half. Leeds were out of the League Cup, and I went back to grappling with the problem of how to persuade a load of spotty fourteen-year-old boys that they needed to know about land use patterns in Brazil.

A couple of weeks later, I had another good reason not to get up early for the daily crawl to Wakefield. Once a month, we were excused attendance at our schools to touch base back at the University Department of

Education. I was in a tutorial group of about twenty students. Earlier in the year, we would meet every week, but now we were down to just once a month. I didn't enjoy almost everything about that course, but the tutorials were the bits I didn't enjoy the most.

Every other member of the group was a gung-ho supercreep who apparently thought the Theory of Education was the most fascinating topic imaginable. We would be expected to read vast chunks of viciously dull text before each tutorial. Everyone else would invariably have done all the reading and be prepared to join in the tedious discussions that we would have. They all made me, who had not actually got round to doing the reading and did not really have any opinion on the psychology of learning or whatever, look like a right waster. Which of course was exactly what I was, but if there had been any others even a bit like that in the group, I wouldn't have looked so bad.

Worse still, not only did they make me look bad in front of the tutor, who was a nice enough old buffer who didn't seem to mind too much whether I could be bothered to do the work, they also all clearly regarded me like something smelly and unwelcome they had just discovered on the sole of their shoe.

So anyway, I had a day off teaching so I could go to this almost as excruciating tutorial. The only plus was that I did not have to get up so early. I was still in bed, awake but not yet up (and actually wondering how late I could justifiably be for the thing) when I heard a motor bike coming up the road. This was a perfectly normal occurrence, but something made me sit up and look out of the window. I saw the bike stop and a uniformed man get off and walk up to our door.

It was a telegram.

It was for me!

HAPPY TO OFFER YOU JOB AS ATH DIRECTOR AMERICAN SCHOOL TANGIER PLSE ANSWER ASAP. MCALLISTER.

Wow!

At the tutorial, the tutor started on about how important it was that we start thinking about our careers. "In fact," he said, "I think it would be a good idea if we quickly went around the table and each of you shared where you are in the job process."

Plain girl with very thick glasses: "Well, I've written to twenty-seven schools, and I've been offered an interview at a comprehensive in Burnley."

Dumpy girl with greasy hair: "I had an interview for a job teaching delinquent children at a special school in Salford, but I don't know if I'll get called back for a second interview because there were over fifty candidates."

Etc., etc... until it came round to me. Twenty pairs of arrogant and hostile eyes turned to me. Arrogant, hostile, and also a little amused. They were all waiting for something from me they could snicker about over their coffee afterwards. 'I knew that Rob wouldn't have got anywhere in the job search.' 'As if anyone would ever give HIM a job.'

I waited for a couple of seconds, and then, as cool as fuck, I said, as casually as I could manage, "I've been offered the post of Athletic Director at The American School of Tangier."

Into the shocked silence that followed, I tossed in "That's in Morocco."

A one-man pack of hyenas

All the reputable International Schools around the world include in their package, as a minimum, the price of an air ticket out to their location from your home country. The American School of Tangier, on the other hand, just expected you to present yourself at their door on the required date, and how you got there was deemed to be entirely your own affair. Which was why I hitch-hiked from Leeds to Morocco. On the ferry from Algeciras to Tangier, I struck up a conversation with a young English lad called Brian. He was on his way to Agadir where he was going to teach wind-surfing.

By the time the ship had steamed round the headland to give us our first glimpse of Tangier, with its wide sweeping sandy bay and the minarets and ancient castle walls of the city climbing the lower slopes of the hill at the far end, we had agreed to share a room on arrival, and as we stepped onto African soil, we allowed the first pleasant-looking tout to lead us out of the port and through a labyrinth of narrow streets into the medina. Eventually, we arrived at a 'guesthouse', where we were given a boxroom with two beds and a wardrobe.

Within half an hour of our arrival, a knock came at the door and a particularly shady character allowed himself into the room.

"Hey, man. Wanna buy some hash?" he said, producing a large brown slab wrapped in paper like a French cheese. "This good stuff, man. This the best. Get you real high. I make good price for you."

Before I could reply with a firm, 'No, thank you very much. Not today, my good man'. Brian got in first with, "How much, then?"

Even though I was a tyro in Morocco, I already sensed this was an error. Later, I would learn how right I was; rule number one when confronted with somebody trying to sell you something in Morocco is if you evince the slightest degree of interest in the product then you are lost. A Moroccan street hawker is like a one-man pack of hyenas, and you are a wildebeest. An expression of even the mildest interest in the wares is the equivalent of the wildebeest showing the hyaena it is limping. The trader will swarm all over you, circling you, nipping away at you, now from this angle, now from that, until you finally sink in a heap to the ground, defeated and defenceless, and give the infuriating beast five dirhams for his stupid cigarette lighter or coca-cola frisbee or lime-green sunhat or whatever.

So "How much then?" was not, tactically speaking, a good response. He was also staring at the slab as if it was pure gold or chocolate or something.

"Tell you what. You try little. You like, I give you good price, Okay?"

And with that, our guest quickly broke off a few crumbs and expertly prepared a joint. He lit it, and passed it to Brian.

Brian took a long drag and, holding it deep in his lungs, offered it to me. I shook my head, but he waved it at me encouragingly, whilst his eyes were spinning like clothes in a washing machine. I took it, but didn't take a drag.

"Is good, eh?" asked Mohamed. (Shall we call him?)

Brian finally exhaled. He took the joint back from me. "Yes, it is good," he said with enthusiasm, and took another drag.

"So how much you want?"

"Well, how much would it be for a piece of that slab?"

Mohamed indicated with his finger about half of it, and said "This much, one thousand dollars."

This was ridiculous! Even I, who was not, at that time, into drugs at all, knew that this was ridiculous.

"That's ridiculous!" said Brian. He had been led to believe that hash was as cheap as slightly carbonated water in Morocco, and here he was being asked to pay ten times more than he would in England.

"I tell you, this good stuff. Okay, how about this." He moved his finger. "Five hundred?"

I was beginning to feel uneasy.

Mohamed was now fully in pack-of-hyenas mode. No matter how much Brian told him that a) his prices were ridiculous, and b) he didn't have that much money anyway (and neither did I, I added hastily when he glanced at one point in my direction), Mohamed closed in for the kill. His demeanour had rapidly switched from our smiling buddy who wanted nothing more than to make us happy by supplying us with his heavenly hashish to an impatient, snarling, vexed trader who clearly felt he had fulfilled his side of a bargain and now expected his due reward.

And finally, he pounced.

"Okay," he said, wrapping up his slab and slipping it into his pocket, "you no want any of this. So that's just one hundred dollars."

"What for?"

"You smoke joint, you must pay."

The next few minutes were ugly. Moroccans, I later learned, are very good at feigning a murderous, affronted fury. Mohamed was particularly talented at it. He was assisted, for the murderous bit, by a very convincing prop: the knife with which he had cut the slab, and which he now made a point of producing again.

All three men in the room were now fully aware of exactly what was going on. The whole thing was a well-rehearsed charade designed to bully and frighten innocent and unwary (yet greedy) tourists fresh off the ferry into handing over a nice wodge of cash. It was a pretty good scam, and we, well no, I have to say in my defence that it was actually Brian, had fallen for it hook, line and sinker.

Finally, after what seemed like at least an hour of angry dispute, we persuaded Mohamed to leave. But we weren't off the hook. Only by dint of emptying out the entire contents of our backpacks, had we managed to persuade him of the true fact that we didn't actually have any ready money at all. All we had were traveller's cheques, which we were intending to cash in the morning. Mohamed made it perfectly clear that he, and his knife, and probably several of his more burly friends, would be back very soon after the banks opened, and if we didn't pay up then, we could expect things to get really nasty.

We were in a hole.

Obviously, we had to get out of the guesthouse since that was where Mohamed would come looking for us in the morning. But, even if we'd wanted to just cut our losses and pay for our room and leave straightaway, we couldn't; we had no cash. We had been in the room for at least a couple of hours, and there was no way they would let us just walk out with all our stuff without paying something.

After some discussion, we came up with a plan.

We repacked our backpacks, and carried them down to the toilet at the end of the corridor. This room, we had found, had a small window overlooking a back alley. The window was small, but just about large enough for our purposes. Brian locked himself in the toilet, while I went downstairs and sauntered casually out of the door. Once in the street, I walked up and down, pretending to look into the shops, until I discovered a likely looking alleyway. I ducked down it, rounded a corner, and looked up. There were a number of windows , but it was easy to see which one was the right one ; it was the one with the backpack stuffed halfway out of it. I called up to Brian to push it out, which he did, and I managed to catch the thing as it fell. The other pack soon followed, and I set off with them back up the alley, turned away from the guesthouse, and made my way swiftly through the winding streets, hoping furiously that Mohamed hadn't left any of his friends outside the place to follow us if we ran.

Eventually, after a lot of twisting and turning and taking the most roundabout route I could manage without getting completely lost, I arrived back at the entrance to the ferry port. I was extremely hot after over an hour's walking carrying two heavy packs. I sat down, leaned my back against a pillar, and waited. I had just managed to get rid of my thirty-fourth annoying person who wanted to help me find a guesthouse/sell me something/be my guide when a breathless Brian turned up. He had followed our plan of waiting in the room for a while before copying my casual just-off-out-to-look-at-the-shops saunter past the guesthouse owner and then legging it for our rendezvous point.

Ignoring all further offers of help (and we had a few), we walked resolutely into the new part of town and checked into a solid and respectable hotel which we could not afford. As we passed the bus station, a particularly shady young man, seeing us heading from the port, tried one of the standard opening lines which the street pests of the city used to engage their prey: "Welcome to Tangier!"

"How's the activities programme looking?"

I didn't have the highest expectations for my career as Athletic Director of the American School of Tangier.

Given that I was not properly trained to teach PE, and given that I knew next to nothing about American sports, I felt a total fraud and I expected to be found out within weeks and sent packing. The most I hoped for was that when they fired me, they would at least give me enough money for me to survive while I hitched back to England.

Nevertheless, that is not to say that I wasn't prepared to give it my best shot.

Fortunately, there was a Japanese woman called Mrs Hoopschrauber (she had a Swiss husband) who taught PE to all the really little ones. My job was to teach Grades 4–8 (i.e. age 9–13), to organize an after-school activities programme for the older kids, and to coach and/or arrange games and tournaments for various school teams.

I found the actual teaching bit quite easy. I did have a bit of a bank of activities I could use, and I developed a method of learning as I went along. I was very concerned that I maintained my credibility with the kids, though, so the system would go something like this:

Kids repetitively at the beginning of first class: "Can we play kickball?"

Me (thinking: Kickball?! What the hell is that?): "No."

Next class... same thing.

Etc., etc.

Me, at the beginning of fifth class: "Right, today we're going to play kickball. I would like two volunteers to get the equipment out and set it up while the rest of us warm up."

(After seeing the kids set up bases in a diamond and place a football in the middle, guessing that it is a kicking version of baseball, but not being sure of all the baseball rules) "Okay, Mark and Tommy, pick two teams and get your positions sorted out."

Etc., etc. If ever I found my lack of knowledge exposed, I always had the perfect out: "Ah, well I'm playing British rules, but if you know that way then we'd better stick to that."

Organising the activities programme was much more daunting. I was told that I had to contact all the other teachers and persuade them to offer lots of exciting things for the kids to do after school. This was a very difficult thing to do. Firstly, I was terrified of all the other teachers as they were real adults (I still felt like a big kid) and were proper teachers. Secondly, none of them, for some peculiar reason, seemed to show any enthusiasm for doing something which would mean more work for them, but for which they wouldn't get paid.

And thirdly, they were all Americans.

And they're a funny lot, are the Americans. The fellow who taught English approached me on Day One and informed me that he would be coaching the basketball team. The vaguest shadow of the thought flitted across my mind to reply, "Excuse me. I am the Athletic Director, and it is *I* who will decide who will and who will not be coaching the basketball team. If you wish to be considered for the position, please make your application in writing, and I will let you know of my decision in due course." But in fact, flooded with relief that it looked like I had at least one activity nailed down, I said "Okay, right, yeah, great."

A couple of days later, he bumped into me again and said that for his practices he would be needing some 'jump ropes'.

What the hell is a jump rope?

A rope you suspend from the ceiling for people to jump up and try to touch?

Seemed possible, since I knew that jumping high was a big skill in basketball. "Oh. I'm sorry, we haven't got any."

He looked at me suspiciously. He was your classic American English teacher; young, scruffy, prone to wearing check shirts and corduroy trousers, longish unkempt hair, probably from New England. He was also brusque and confident, a confidence born, I felt, from the fact that he was screwing a beautiful eleventh grade American girl who lived in the dorm (AST was like that). "Are you sure? We had some last year. What's happened to them?"

"I don't know. They must have been thrown out, I suppose, over the summer."

He gave me a fishy look, may well have said "Hmph," and walked away. I immediately went to my office, which doubled as the equipment storage room, and rummaged through all the boxes of useless old stuff, which had evidently been accumulating there for decades, but I couldn't find any sign of any ropes which could be hung from the ceiling. If he ever asked me for odd boxing gloves, broken lacrosse sticks, or fencing masks for one of his practices, though, I was happy to learn that I would be able to provide him with a good supply.

The next afternoon, he held his first practice, and I was intrigued to notice, as I walked by to see how things were going, that all the players were skipping, using the skipping ropes which the coach must have marched into my office and taken himself.

Lisa was another English teacher, or rather, she was another American who was teaching English. She, like me, was starting her first job and was dead keen. When I asked her if she could offer anything after school, she replied that she would love to start a 'riding club'. I didn't like the sound of that. I had no idea where or even if there were any riding stables in Tangier. How would we get the kids there and back? Would I be blamed if a kid got hurt?

"Hmm," I replied. "Where would you run this activity?"

"In my classroom."

"Right. Great." I was floundering, sensing that there was something I wasn't quite getting. "So... you'd just be working on the theoretical side?"

"Oh no. It would be a chance for the students to do any kind of riding they wanted to."

"Okay. Right, that sounds great."

I decided to go away and think about this, and see if I could make any sense at all. I went into the main office and found a note in my pigeon hole from McAllister, asking me to see him as soon as it was convenient so we could review the progress I was making with the after-school activities programme. McAllister was a big bluff fellow, who could be tremendously genial but, I had already learned, had a very short and fearsome temper. He had remarkable blue eyes which twinkled merrily when he was enjoying cheerful banter with you, but which somehow blazed terrifyingly under his scowling brow when he was angry. His office was the very next room, and the door was open, but I managed to scuttle past it without him calling me in, and went back to my office where I took a piece of paper and sat at my desk. AFTER-SCHOOL ACTIVITIES PROGRAMME, I wrote on the top of the sheet, and underlined it. After a few seconds of careful pondering, I underlined it again. Then I made two columns, headed ACTIVITY and TEACHER.

1. Football   Rob Heath

2. Basketball   Mike Whitlow

3. Riding   Lisa Hope

After a few more minutes of thought, I added (Soccer) after Football, and put a question mark after

Riding, took a deep breath, and set off to show the fruits of my labours to the headmaster.

"Ah Bob. How's the Activities Program looking? We need to get going on getting the kids signed up. Frank always used to have a meeting with the kids on the second day of school." Frank was my predecessor, a man who, by all accounts, was the paragon of Athletic Directors and indeed of human beings in general. Everybody at AST, including the kids, the teachers, the parents, the secretaries, the gardeners, probably even the bloody toilet fittings, *loved* Frank, and from the descriptions I had heard of his qualities, I guessed that he had left to take up a joint position as head of the International Olympic Commission and Secretary-General of the UN.

"Oh right. Well, I am almost ready to do that."

"We need a nice wide range of different activities. What have you got so far?"

"Well, I've got er, three, but I haven't–"

"Three? You're gonna need a damn site more than that. This is a very important programme for this school. You must have more than three. Have you spoken to Lisa? She told me she wanted to start a literary magazine. That could be one."

He blustered on, but I wasn't really paying attention any more. A literary magazine? Oh, it was a WRITING club.

"Is that the list of what you've got?" McAllister was saying, pointing at the paper I held in my hand.

"No. No, this is just... another list."

46

"Hmmph." He scowled suspiciously at the piece of paper. "Well, you can put me down for drama, of course. Now I think you'd better get round and see every teacher before the end of the day and get them all signed up for something."

Eventually, I did get a comprehensive list of offerings together, met with all the kids, and got them all signed up for one thing or another. Most of them stopped meeting after the first couple of sessions, which was fine by both the teachers and the students. As the supervisor of the programme, I really should have insisted they continue, but I soon learned that at AST, the reality of what actually went on was irrelevant as long as things looked good on paper. As long as McAllister, strolling down the corridor with prospective parents or benefactors, could show them a bulletin board with an impressive list of after-school activities displayed, he was happy.

I took care of the football team.

I had a fine bunch of lads who loved to play and were quite talented. They weren't really interested in training or being coached, though, and I reluctantly gave up on those sessions quite early on. I also found to my relief that I didn't have to do anything to organize games. It turned out that we had just about the only proper grass pitch in Tangier except for the one at the stadium, and so just about every school and club in the city wanted to play us. There was a steady stream of people who would walk into school and ask to set up a game.

Some of the behaviour of these visiting teams was appalling in the early days − general cheating such as fouls and dives, disputing refereeing decisions, foul language. I quickly learned, though, that our status as the Wembley of Tangier gave me immense leverage in controlling any bad sportsmanship. During about the third or fourth game we played, I got so annoyed by the antics of the other team that I simply stopped the game, told them to leave, and informed them that they would never be invited back. After that, it was incredible how word evidently passed around amongst the local football fraternity, because from then on visiting teams were always impeccably behaved and exaggeratedly polite. If ever a particularly volatile player should show any signs of reacting to a decision or incident, he would be instantly enveloped by calming, maniacally grinning teammates who would usher him away.

My role consisted of picking the team, encouraging the players to play in their positions and to a system, and reffing the games. I would tell the opposition quite openly that I intended to coach my team at the same time as reffing, and it turned out to be an excellent arrangement because I would be right in the middle of the action and did not have to rely on bellowing things from the touchline as most coaches do. Once the Whatever-You-Do-Don't-Antagonise-The-Crazy-Englishman era began, none of our opponents ever had any problem with this dual role. I was of course scrupulously fair, although I must admit that my players didn't get whistled offside very often. (Because I always yelled at them to get onside before I ever needed to penalise them for it.)

There was one visiting team whose forbearance was tested to the limit when I, in my capacity as referee, scored a goal against them.

My boys had won a corner, and, in the absence of any linesmen, it was my habit at corners to station myself just off the pitch beyond the far post so that I could make sure the ball didn't cross the deadball line as it was swung in and at the same time keep an eye on all the argy-bargy in the penalty area. This particular corner was headed out to the edge of the box, straight to the feet of a visiting player who had loads of time and space. Anticipating that he would turn with the ball and probably hoof it clear, I set off to sprint towards the halfway line to try to keep up with play. Normally on such a run after a corner, I would carefully skirt the middle of the box, but I was so sure that this guy was going to clear the ball I set off in a straight line up the pitch. The idiot on the ball managed to miscontrol it so horribly, however, that it squirted away to one of our players, who immediately took a shot at goal. Unfortunately, his shot was flying well wide of the target... until it hit me on the knee and deflected into the net. Since, as we all know, the referee counts as part of the playing surface, I had no option but to sheepishly allow the goal.

Meanwhile, one other activity which I could guarantee would be gathering momentum was Gary McAllister's drama. It was one of the great AST traditions that Gary would put on a play as a finale to the school year, and indeed the AST play was one of the great events of the Tangier social and cultural calendar. Another AST tradition, perhaps not such a great one, was that McAllister would always pick a good-looking boy to play the lead role, and that boy would then become the headmaster's lover.

Towards the end of the year, everything other than the play took a back seat. Important actors would be excused attending classes to rehearse, or even to rest so that they could devote all their energies to rehearsing. The leading actor, in particular, would spend less time in class than he would on one-on-one sessions in the headmaster's office. Perfecting his oral delivery, no doubt.

That year, they put on a version of *Lord of the Flies*, exclusively adapted for the stage by Gary himself. Some people thought that this was a poor choice of play for a co-educational school, given that it contained absolutely no parts at all for girls. Other people thought that this was precisely its great appeal as far as Gary was concerned; that and the fact that the plot required a troop of fresh-limbed young boys to cavort about the stage dressed only in loin-cloths.

One day, right in the middle of the crisis period leading up to the show, when basically the entire school operation had morphed into a drama production company, I was innocently walking into the teachers' lounge when a wild-eyed McAllister emerged from his office, thrust the keys to the school car into my hands, and sent me on a mission into town to collect a costume which had been altered overnight. It never even occurred to him to inquire whether I had a class coming up, although, as luck would have it, I didn't.

This was quite an exciting task for me, getting to drive the slightly swishy school car (a Fiat estate) around the town where hitherto I had always been a pedestrian. I cruised in along the tree-lined boulevards feeling most pleased with myself, arriving at my destination to find a parking spot available right outside a café. A row of cars were parked nose-on to the pavement, and there was one space for me. I ducked up the alley next to the café and found that Gary's hastily-delivered directions were perfect, grabbed the costume from the seamstress, and returned to the car.

At that point, I encountered a problem. The geography of the parking arrangements required me to back out of my space, but I couldn't get the thing into reverse. I later learned that this particular model requires you to raise a little switch on the side of the gear lever before sliding it across and back to engage reverse, but I had never driven a car with such a system before, and whilst I could tell that there must be some such trick required, I had no idea what it could be.

As I sat there, repetitively waggling the gear lever about in the forlorn hope that it would magically just click into reverse, McAllister's parting words echoed around my head (or at least they will in the movie version of this.) "I must have that costume by twelve o'clock, because Aidan needs to try it on and have enough time to send it back if necessary." It was now 11.45 a.m., and even if I left right then I would have to get very lucky with traffic to make it back by twelve o'clock. And if I haven't already conveyed this impression, let me say right here that when Gary McAllister sent you on a mission vital to the outcome of his play, fucking it up would be an extremely ill-advised course of action.

It was incredible! I only drove a car into that city twice in my entire time in Morocco, and both times I ended up sitting in a panic, uselessly fumbling with a recalcitrant lever. If you wrote it in a book, no one would believe it!

There was only one possible way out. I got out of the car and slid a café table and three chairs (luckily unoccupied) out of the way, ignored the cries of the café owner, jumped back in, and drove up onto the pavement, passed carefully and narrowly between two more tables (occupied) and three parked cars and, with a cheery wave to the astonished café population, bounced back down the kerb at the end of the row of cars onto the road and set course for AST.

This incident may have been traumatic, but the memory of it was what saved me from a huge folly a few years later. After I left Morocco, I went to teach in Northern Greece, and I used to occasionally take teams down to Athens for competition. One night during a volleyball tournament, I went out with a few other coaches, and ended up drinking probably more retsina than I should have done. I got split up from the other folk, and somehow found myself out on the streets all on my own at about three a.m. I was miles from my hotel, there were no taxis about, and I needed to be up at seven a.m. to meet the kids and get to the station to catch a train back to Thessaloniki. As I trudged along somewhat ruefully, a car pulled up to the kerb just in front of me, and the driver leapt out and ran into a bar, leaving the engine running. I was immediately hit by the tempting thought that if I were to get in that car, I could drive it back to my hotel, leave it around the corner in a back street, be happily snuggled up in my bed within fifteen minutes, and nobody would be any the wiser. But luckily, tired and addled though I was, I had just enough mentis still compus to notice that the car was parked right up behind another, and the vision of me sitting at the wheel desperately trying to engage reverse gear when the owner re-emerged was enough to resign me to continuing my sad two hour walk. As I plodded on, though, I imagined the scenarios of how things might have played out if the kids had all turned up at the station in the morning only to find that Mr. Heath was not there because he was in jail for drunken car theft.

But anyway, back in Tangier, the much-vaunted American School production of *Lord of the Flies* was not quite the huge success that the town's literati had been anticipating.

I had been dragooned into helping backstage, and was therefore perfectly placed to watch the drama unfold, and the drama I am talking about now had nothing to do with William Golding's story about a group of boys marooned on a desert island.

Things started to go awry quite early when Aidan Butterworth, Gary's golden boy (that year) who was playing the part of Jack, the leader of the loincloth-clad hunters, realised that he had left the trousers which he wore in his early scenes in McAllister's office. Can't imagine how that had happened, but anyway, he raced off to get them as the opening scenes (which did not include him) were playing. He arrived back in plenty of time before he was due to go on, but he was in such a panic, as he clambered into the trousers, that he mistook a line spoken by Karl Jackson, 'They used to call me Piggy', as 'Please don't call me Piggy', a later line which was his cue to come on. Before anyone could stop him, he marched on stage and delivered his first line.

'Piggy? That's an excellent name for you. Piggy.' The poor startled kids on stage froze, and a ripple of horror almost visibly passed through them. But they all knew that Aidan was, and had to be, the star of the show, and they sensed immediately that the thing to do was to jump ahead and carry on from the point of Jack's entry. I ushered Jack's choirboys, or at least those who had their costumes on, onto the stage and told the others to slip discreetly on as soon as they were ready, and somehow they managed to keep the lines flowing more or less in the right sequence.

After a few minutes, everybody calmed down, and things seemed to be going okay again. True, they had missed out quite a large tranche of the play, but we all felt that nobody in the audience was likely to have noticed. And anyway, it was an adaptation of the novel, so it was perfectly feasible for some parts to be missed out. Everybody, actors on stage and those behind the scenes, had their eyes glued to the director and impresario himself, who sat with the guests of honour in the front row. He had a constant relaxed and satisfied smile on his lips, designed to convey to all and sundry that this magnificent performance, which he knew even outdid last year's hugely acclaimed *The Tempest*, was proceeding exactly as rehearsed. But when the foulup occurred, poor Aidan saw a look of such burning fury in his eyes it was remarkable that he did not turn to a pile of ashes on the spot. Now, though, McAllister's eyes had regained their serenity, and everybody relaxed.

Shortly afterwards, just as I was double-checking the props for scene fourteen, the backstage door burst open and McAllister stood there with thunderous brow. "What about the fucking conch, you morons?" he hissed in a somewhat un-headmasterly manner. The conch was a massive seashell which Piggy finds in a lagoon, and which comes to play a symbolic role in the group meetings the boys have. My first thought was that Gary had somehow thought that we had lost the shell we were using as the conch, so I replied calmly, "It's there, on the table."

He strode towards me and, bringing his furious face right up to mine, and desperately fighting the urge to shout, he said, "And when is Piggy going to find it?"

As he continued, ranting wildly about what a disaster this was, I realised what he was on about. The part of the text we had missed out included the finding of the conch, and its designation as the signifier of who was allowed to speak at meetings.

I could see that this was a significant omission, but thought that it wasn't such an insurmountable problem. The same idea obviously occurred to Lisa Hope, who was the prompter. "Let's just leave out all references to the conch then," she offered. McAllister wheeled on her, just managed to stop himself from hitting her, and at that point the inner battle he had been fighting between the urge to vent his fury and the need to remember that there was a very important audience just a few feet away on the other side of a thin wooden board was conclusively lost.

He shouted at her, "We can't do that you stupid bitch! What about Jonathan's line?"

As I watched the audience stirring uncomfortably through my peephole, I realised why Gary was so worked up, and why this problem was not so easy to solve. Jonathan, an insignificant little weed who at that moment was cowering behind the curtain, was the son of Winston Courtney, the United States Consul-General in Tangier. Jonathan had neither the talent nor the motivation to be in the school play, but McAllister had decided early in the piece that even though those qualities were absent, as indeed were pretty well every other quality you might think of, he did possess one attribute which made him an irreplaceable member of the cast; his parentage. Right now, Courtney was sitting in the seat next to the one recently vacated by McAllister, where he was pleasantly anticipating the arrival on stage of the pride of his loins, and the delivery of the one line Jonathan had been allowed to have. Near the end of the play, when Jack takes his troupe and flounces out of a meeting of all the boys, Jonathan was to say, 'Jack shouldn't have spoken if he wasn't holding the conch!'

It was one of those classic situations that only the theatre can bring us. On the platform, a dozen or so teenagers manfully strove to hold the thing together, calling out their lines and moving about the stage as they had been directed to do. Behind the scenes, total bedlam prevailed as everybody struggled to come up with an idea to solve the problem which, as the moment for Jonathan's line drew closer, was becoming more and more acute. Gary was furiously thinking, pounding his head in an effort to force it to produce an idea. His first thought had been to give Jonathan someone else's line, but that plan was aborted even before Lisa had found a suitable replacement as soon as he saw the look of abject terror in the boy's face. It had taken weeks to imprint the words of his one pathetic line into what passed for his brain, and the idea of starting all over again with a new one was, we all realised, a complete non-starter. Other suggestions came in from various quarters, but they were all rejected with increasingly demented and audible responses, until he finally came up with a plan he felt would suit.

"Heath!" he called to me. "Look in the costume hamper and find something that will fit me. I'm going to have to sort this goddamn mess out myself."

When he had called my name, I feared he was going to send me out on stage, so it was with some relief that I began to ferret through the heap of old costumes. I knew from what I could hear on stage that I had very little time, though, and so I grabbed the first thing I found that looked like it might fit Gary's ample frame and chucked it across to him.

It was a long, frilly Victorian dress.

Reading his face at that point, I really thought he was going to totally lose it for a moment. I swear he was on the verge of crossing the room and throttling me with that dress, but then he heard from the stage Ralph announce that the critical meeting of the boys was about to begin. Frantically, he threw off his jacket and trousers and started to struggle into the dress, shouting at anybody near him to do him up at the back.

It would be difficult to assess whether the cast were more astonished than the audience when the meeting of all the boys on the island was suddenly interrupted by the arrival on stage of the Headmaster wearing a long floral dress and with a blonde wig, which he'd grabbed from the costume hamper on his way on, perched on his head.

There was a moment of stunned silence before Gary, attempting an old crone's voice, came out with "Boys! Fear not! I am, er ... Victoria, an old woman who has been shipwrecked on this island for years. I've been secretly watching you, and er, and I've noticed that your meetings are toadally undemocradic." (He was slipping back into his New England prep school master's voice.) "I suggest that you use this..." At this point, he realised that he had forgotten to take the conch on with him. Divining what he was trying to do, I had just noticed the same thing. I grabbed it from the table and skilfully slid it across the stage so that it landed right at his feet. Unfortunately, my brilliance was wasted because it was at just that point that he turned to me in panic and hissed, "Pass me the conch!"

I pointed frantically at his feet and hissed back, "It's there! It's there!"

He pirouetted wildly, trying to see what I was pointing at. I'm not sure if he trod on the conch first, or tripped on his dress, but the outcome was that he hit the stage with a massive thump, his skirts billowing up to display to the audience exactly what the fashionable castaway old crone was wearing for underwear that year; black shoes, grey socks and purple boxers.

He clambered back to his feet, grabbing some of the parts of the now-shattered shell. "I suggest that you use this conch, and whomsoever should be holding it is the only one who is allowed to speak," and he hurriedly exited, holding his skirts above his ankles, stage left.

If the silence following his entrance was stunned, that following McAllister's exit was comatose. Eventually, one of the boys on stage managed to summons the wherewithal to come up with a line, and the boys, dutifully clasping the broken bit of conch, managed to shakily continue with the scene, until Jack eschewed the conch and announced that he and his choirboys were going to leave and make their own tribe. This was Jonathan Courtney's big moment... but the line which McAllister had done so much to make possible remained unspoken. Gary and I, in the wings, and all the actors on stage, looked around and realised that Jonathan was not there.

Wearily, the cast, by this point inured to unexpected events, got on with the script. Jack and his followers marched off, and Ralph and Piggy began discussing what to do next. Suddenly, there came a roar from offstage. "GET ON THAT STAGE AND SAY YOUR GODDAMN LINE!" and a petrified Jonathan came flying onstage from the opposite wing to where I was standing. Evidently, the Director had found his absent actor cowering somewhere, and had finally cracked.

"Jack shouldn't have spoken if he wasn't holding the conch!" faltered the poor boy.

"Curtain! Curtain!" cried McAllister, who had obviously had enough. I undid the toggle and down came the curtain on what I think we will have to describe as a very loose adaptation of *Lord of the Flies*. The applause was bemused and muted at first, but a few of Gary's chums rallied round and pepped things up, and soon enough the cast were taking their third curtain call, with Jonathan Courtney being reluctantly pushed to the front for a special bow, and then the audience filed out and set off for the famous after-show party at Gary's house where all agreed it had been a magnificent production, even outdoing last year's *The Tempest*.

Strangely, nobody mentioned the fact that the actor who played Victoria had not come out to take a bow.

It was very nice to get paid for doing my favourite thing

I was astonished to learn, shortly after my arrival in Tangier, that my reputation had preceded me. Well actually, and this was the problem really, the reputation of somebody who I actually wasn't had preceded me.

I have already explained how, without actually lying or even distorting the truth (much), I allowed Mr McAllister, at my interview in London, to form the impression that I was a top class young footballer. Hearing that I had played on a National Champion college soccer team (as he no doubt put it when he was touting my talents on his return after recruiting me), he evidently assumed that I would have been playing professionally by now if I hadn't decided to take up teaching, probably due to my love of pedagogy.

I learned later, as I came to know McAllister and his school, that image was everything to him. The school was in actuality a terribly shabbily run institution, but as long as it had a veneer of class about it, and all his rich chums in the city, who of course never actually came to see any classes taught, were impressed by flashy extravaganzas like the play or the graduation ceremony, McAllister was happy.

Which is why, I also only figured out later, he took a punt on a young English lad with no appropriate training or experience and offered him the job as Athletic Director. Because Tangier had a very high profile football team, and McAllister quite correctly reasoned that if his Athletic Director was starring with them it would constitute a tremendous feather in the school's cap.

But there was one major flaw in his cunning plan; I was not the brilliant young footballer he imagined me to be.

I was quite a good player. And I certainly loved the game with a passion. It had always been my dream to be a star, and to one day pull on the white shirt of Leeds United and lead the club to the triumphs which I had seen them denied so cruelly from the terraces when they had been the greatest team in the world in the early 70s. But I had gradually come to the sad realisation in my late teens that I just wasn't good enough. I would have settled for a career slogging away in the Third Division for Doncaster Rovers or Hartlepool, actually, but I apparently wasn't even that good.

Actually, I always harboured an inner belief that I *was* good enough, but that I had not got the breaks, and I had been the victim of a cruel conspiracy to prevent me fulfilling my potential. The perpetrators of this conspiracy were my parents and one stupid little bastard who lived in Surrey.

My parents' role in the affair was that, after a brilliant football career at Primary School in Harrogate, culminating in selection for the town team, they took the inconceivably ill-judged decision to send me to Ashville College. This was a very bad decision on many levels, the most important being that there were no girls at Ashville; but that's not relevant right now. The other massive reason why this was a huge blunder was that Ashville is a rugby-playing school.

So, just at the time when I should have been refining my skills, and building on that immense early potential, I was placed instead into the hands of Jeff Ould. This man was a Welsh international hooker [Note to my American readers, in the unlikely event that such an animal should exist: a 'hooker' here refers to the name of a position on a rugby team.] who had been brought onto the staff at Ashville allegedly as a Chemistry teacher but his real remit was to raise the standard of the school's rugby teams. As such, he was put in charge of the First XV and the under 12s, presumably with the reasoning that he could get the young'uns moving in the right direction straight from the kick-off, as it were.

Even if Jeff Ould had been the most inspiring coach in the world, and rugby a thrilling and engaging sport, I don't think the scowl on my face due to the fact that we weren't playing football would ever have left. As it was, I found rugby to be a brutal and mindless pastime which seemed to mainly involve scrabbling about in freezing puddles of mud and a vast amount of unseemly grappling. And Ould's sarcastic approach, arrogant attitude and Welsh accent didn't help matters.

Finally, I was released from this rugger hell when my dad was transferred to a post in London. Whilst this meant leaving my beloved Leeds United behind, the upside was that I switched to a football school. I was 15 by that time, and I knew that I needed to get spotted by a professional scout pretty damn quick, but at least I could now see a route ahead of me. I walked straight into the new school's First XI, and by the second year was selected to go for trials for the Surrey schools' team. If I could get into their squad, I would go to the English School's Football Festival in Skegness which everybody knew was purely a shop window for the professional game. As I had heard it told, kids played their games in front of throngs of scouts from the top clubs, who could barely be restrained from rushing onto the pitch to thrust contracts under the noses of any player with any ability. Glen Hoddle, Kevin Keegan, Bryan Robson... they had all been spotted at Skegness.

So that trial was my big, big chance. And that was where the stupid little bastard who lived in Surrey entered the plot.

We were all placed randomly into teams and off we went. My game kicked off, and the ball was played back to a kid in midfield who hoofed it high over my head down the pitch. In my highly motivated and excited state, and desperate to impress watching selectors, I immediately hared after it, even though I clearly could not get to it before the opposition left back. The ball bounced once, and the left back approached it, but I think he was taken aback by how fast I was onto him, because rather than take the ball down as he looked like he was going to do, he suddenly swung his foot through it and smacked it back where it had come from. The ball travelled about two feet from the boot of the stupid little bastard before burying itself deep into my goolies.

Anyone who has experienced such a thing knows that your innards feel like blancmange for a horrible period, and you just want to crawl away and be left to seep into the earth somewhere, and then after a period it all starts to go away and you still feel a bit tender but you can start to function again slowly. But on that day, the blow was so severe I was completely done for. I never got back on the pitch.

But I had just about recovered when, during one of my first few days teaching at AST, a guy appeared and asked me to go for a trial with Renaissance Sportive de Tanger. RST at that time were ironically in a very similar state to that which my favourites Leeds United were in; a once-great side which had fallen on hard times, suffered an unthinkable relegation, and were now languishing in the lower division from which they just could not seem to extricate themselves.

It turned out that my timetable had classes early and late but a big gap in the middle, and that gap just happened to coincide with RST's training time. (Coincidence? I thought later. Perhaps not.) So the following day I jumped in a taxi and headed up to the Renaissance stadium, the Merlain.

It was an impressive bowl with concrete rows acting as seats, except for a big nobs section at the halfway line where there were comfy wooden seats with cushions. A man in a suit was waiting for me, and I was ushered in to a changing room, and greeted shyly and reverently by a group of lads who clearly thought a star had arrived in their midst.

Out on the pitch, a strange thing happened. I don't know if it was something to do with the high expectations of the players, but I found myself temporarily transformed into the very player they thought I was. I had read about top players in various sports suddenly finding themselves in a cocoon wherein they could do nothing wrong, and for a few tantalizingly brief moments, I knew what that was like.

I jogged out across the track and onto the pitch, and joined a few players already out there, who were knocking a few balls about. One lad invited me to go down the other end of the pitch. He passed me a ball and then ran down the touchline. I hit a pass out in front of him, which skidded across the turf and held up beautifully right in his path without him having to break stride, and then ran on myself towards the box. He took a couple more touches, then hit a pass across to me. I met it on the second bounce as I ran and tried a shot on the half volley. (Normal likely Heath outcome for such a manoeuvre: ball clears bar by ten feet, or screws miserably wide.) I caught it perfectly, and the ball fizzed like an arrow into the top corner of the net.

I remained in this incredible zone for several minutes. Scarcely believing what was happening to me, I continued to convert a variety of crosses from Hassan (as I later learned he was called) with unerring aplomb, peppering the (admittedly unguarded) net with headers, smacking volleys in with either foot, and sometimes flicking the ball up first before driving it home.

Of course, it was too good to last.

The coach, a peculiar middle-aged man who was from Bulgaria and spoke to us in execrable French which was nevertheless somehow very comprehensible, called us over and sent us off to run two laps of the track. After a number of gruelling fitness drills under the torrid sun, we finally made contact with the balls again, and I found that my magic touch had gone.

It had been a wonderful interlude, allowing me to feel what it must have been like to be Allan Clarke, but I think, strangely enough, it was the cause of my downfall as a Renaissance Sportive player. The other players, having expected a superstar, and then seen me casually burying crosses into the net with such panache, were clearly hugely disappointed in my efforts when I revealed my true abilities. And this disappointment, curiously, had a drastic effect on my confidence.

I continued to turn up every day for training, and was named in the squad for games, but I never really played anywhere near my normal level. I turned out in front of thousands of people, but that didn't bother me at all. It was the feeling that my teammates did not have total confidence in me which undermined me. The standard was high. This was the second tier of a country who qualified for the World Cup not too many years later. One player in particular, Rubio, was unbelievably talented. He had played for RST as a youngster and then gone off for a few years to play in Belgium. But apparently, he couldn't settle there, and just after I started playing, he arrived back to huge acclaim from the Renaissance fans. He was a tiny, quicksilver midfielder with incredibly quick and deft feet. Even in this elevated company, though, I believe if I had played at my best I could have held my own. But the sense that the other lads didn't really rate me gnawed away at my confidence; my touch was shaky, my passing awry, and my shooting woeful.

I made the sixteen for most games, but was always on the bench, and I only got a very few sporadic minutes of actual playing time. Nevertheless, the experience gave me a very interesting insight into the psychology of the substitute.

Conflicting emotions! You want the team to do well so you can get the win bonus which we were (ostensibly) paid; but you want the team to do badly so the coach will have to shake things up. If a player in your position goes down injured, you hope it's not serious, because he's a friend and colleague who you train with every day; but you hope it is serious enough for him to be unable to continue. (And if it were to keep him out for the next few weeks, you wouldn't mind that much.) You desperately want to get out there, convinced that you can make a difference and win the game for the team; but you are also terrified of being thrown on and then making a mistake before you are properly attuned to the game and costing your team the match. You spend half your time watching the match, and the other half watching the coach out of the corner of your eye, trying to assess how he is feeling, his mood, his opinion on how things are going. Occasionally, the coach will cast his gaze along the bench. Why is he doing that? Is he contemplating a change, and wondering which of the gumbies he has at his disposal might be able to make a difference?

All these feelings run through your head, and you know full well that all the other guys are feeling the same thing, but you have to maintain a façade of total positive support of the team. If we go a goal behind early on, it is good, in a way, see above, for the subs, because the chances of one of them being needed have to be a little higher. But of course, none of you can show any elation at all; you have to affect total dismay and dejection.

[There was an incident in English football a few years ago when a manager spotted his sub keeper laughing just after his team had conceded a goal, and he cuffed him around the head. I knew exactly what that was all about!]

At halftime, the playing eleven would troop off to the changing room and listen to a pidgin tirade from Bollokov, and the subs would go out on the pitch and knock a ball about. Occasionally, the brilliant Bulgar would decide to make a change at half-time, and in such a case, he would dispatch Hamid, the one-eyed, crippled, hunch-backed (but apart from that he was in great shape) kitman, to the pitch to summons the chosen sub. The problem was that Hamid was not the fastest mover, and he had to go out of the tunnel, across the track, across the javelin area behind the goal, and finally onto the pitch, before he could deliver his message. So we would be flicking the ball about between us, trying not to think that thousands of bored people were watching us merely because they had nothing else to do, and at the same time we would each be trying not to show each other that we were all keeping an eye out for any sign of Hamid emerging from the tunnel. On the rare occasions when he did appear, the wait while he hobbled towards us was agonising, and the disappointment (mixed with a little bit of relief) when he finally indicated who had been chosen was terrible.

It was very nice to get paid for doing my favourite thing. My salary at the American School was less than paltry, and with Renaissance I was purportedly given quite a substantial monthly sum plus weekly bonuses if I was in the squad and we won. Unfortunately, the football money quite frequently failed to materialise. There were all kinds of shenanigans going on behind the scenes, with boardroom manoeuvring and takeovers and fatcat financiers who never actually came up with the moolah. We as players heard all kinds of rumours (most of which passed me by because I didn't pick up on what everyone was saying), but for us the bottom line was that sometimes we got paid, sometimes we only got a proportion of what we were due, and sometimes we got sincere apologies and promises we would get what we were owed next month.

But in the end, it was the ennui, not the financial irregularity, that did for my career as a (semi, but I usually omit that bit) professional footballer.

Constantly humming

One of the several terrifyingly intimidating directives I was given by McAllister when I started my job was to organise some contests and exchanges with our counterpart school down in the Moroccan capital, the Rabat American School. "And I want you to make sure that we whup them at a few things this year as well!" he added threateningly.

New to teaching, new to directing athletics, and new to Morocco, this assignment seemed hopelessly impossible to accomplish, so I adopted a policy which seemed to be the best option: ignore the whole thing and hope it would go away. Unfortunately, this policy didn't work. After a few weeks, the clamouring from the kids about when will we be playing Rabat began to be echoed by the Big Man himself, who would ask, every time he caught sight of me, why I hadn't contacted them yet.

So eventually, with great trepidation, I went up to the office in one of my free periods, asked for the RAS number, and dialled it. I fully expected the Athletic Director down there to be some overbearing, super-experienced American bully, and my true status as a charlatan would be cruelly exposed, while I inevitably ended up agreeing to do something which would make McAllister go ballistic.

So I was much relieved to hear the engaged signal. I hastily put down the phone and returned to my office.

A few days later, I plucked up the courage to try again, but they were engaged again. They were still engaged on both Monday and Tuesday of the following week. And on every other day as well.

This was mystifying, but also gratifying. I was able to say to McAllister, in all honesty, that I had been trying to call Rabat but I just couldn't get through.

It's hard to know how long this charade would have gone on. It was only months later that I learned, when I was distracted by someone just as I completed dialling a number and so didn't hang up straight away, that a Moroccan phone makes a just-connecting-you sound which is exactly like the British engaged signal, followed a few seconds later by a ringing tone which I had hitherto never waited long enough to hear.

It all became immaterial when there was a knock on my door one Friday night and I opened it to a wild-eyed young man who introduced himself as Kenny Burns, the Athletic Director of the Rabat American School. He was new at the job, had been told that he had to contact me to arrange some exchanges, had been unable to contact me by phone (I never asked him if he found us permanently engaged.) and so had decided to come up to Tangier to meet me in person.

Not only was he patently not an American (he was from Paignton), it turned out that he was certainly neither a bully nor (too much of) a know-it-all.

We went straight out and hit the bars, he ended up staying the night, and we became firm friends and partners-in-crime.

He was a peculiar character, though, old Burnsey. He had the interesting conversational tendency to leap without warning from one subject to another, usually totally unrelated, which meant you had to be constantly on your toes to keep up with him. He also had the strange habit of constantly humming to himself. All the time you were talking to him, he would hum, and he would somehow seem to continue humming even as he was talking back. The hum would still be there in the background, part real, part imaginary, as he spoke, and he would often break off in mid-sentence to throw in a few bars of humming before jumping right back in as if nothing had happened.

Eventually, I grew accustomed to this little tic, and even barely noticed it, but at first I found it most disconcerting. When I got to know him well, I once asked him why he hummed all the time, and he professed not to know what I was talking about.

The morning after his sudden appearance, we sat down and fleshed out plans for a couple of mutual exchanges, and a few weeks later he was back in Tangier on board a bus with twenty-five of his students. We had a fine day of competition in football and volleyball, the RAS kids all dispersed to the homes of AST students I had paired them up with, and Burnsey and I went out on the town again.

Thus was set the blueprint for a series of very successful inter-school competitions. Occasionally, we would throw another school (Casablanca American School, or the Lycée Française) into the mix. They were always events that were exhausting and exhilarating for us in equal measure. We would invariably spend all day ceaselessly engaged with the competition, either coaching or reffing and sometimes both, out in the hot sun, and then would be out carousing until deep into the night. One particularly hot day, we both had worn hats but forgotten to protect our ears and we hit the town that night each sporting a bright red, blistered pair of what we came to call 'AD's ears'.

Burnsey hit upon the excellent idea of writing each other congratulatory letters after each of these things was over, complimenting the host on the exemplary organisation and the hugely rewarding experience the children had had etc. etc., and we copied these to our respective heads and kept them in a file to make us look good. It was a little joke that we tried to outdo each other in the flowery hyperbole of our compliments in each successive letter, but there was usually an element of truth in them as well, because we grew pretty good at running these shows, and the kids did indeed have a great time.

We did make one major mistake, however.

Somehow, I don't know what we can have been thinking about, we scheduled one of these things on the same day as the FA Cup Final!

This was a monumental blunder, because the Cup Final was the only English game that was shown on Moroccan TV all year. After months of dragging ourselves across a football desert, an oasis had finally appeared, and yet we had committed ourselves to staying out in the footie-free dunes reffing Middle School basketball games. By the time we realised our error, it was too late to change the date of the exchange, because the plans of too many other people revolved around the event.

When the AST party arrived in Rabat on the Friday night, at the end of a long and raucous bus journey, Burnsey greeted us effusively, but quickly gave me a wink and muttered quietly, "Don't worry. I've got a plan."

He called all my kids around prior to distributing them to the host families, but first he gave them all a lecture about making sure they got a good night's sleep because they would need to be up early in the morning. As each family left, he made sure to ask the parent if they knew what time their charges were due back at school in the morning. I was wondering what was going on, and then I saw a schedule of events on a poster behind Burnsey's head. I was astonished to read:

06.30 a.m. All players arrive at school

06.40 a.m. First game warmups begin

07.00 a.m. First game (RAS girls v AST girls)

Usually, we would get these things underway around nine thirty or ten, and drag them out all day long, but I saw now that Burnsey's brilliant plan was to get it all started early and have it all done and dusted by 1.30 p.m., giving us enough time to shoot off and watch the Final. He told me later that he had encountered a little griping from parents about this schedule, but had come up with the genius explanation that we had moved everything forward so that the children would not have to compete during the hottest part of the day.

Another regular feature of our exchanges was that everybody would be pretty relaxed about the schedule, and events would invariably get a bit behind as the day wore on, without anyone being particularly concerned. Not this time. Burnsey and I were like concentration camp guards, screaming at kids to get to their games on time. Games started at the scheduled time, even if some of the participants were not all there, and we went to great lengths to make sure they finished on time as well. Since we were both coaches and refs, we made a pact not to call any time-outs. One game looked like it might go into overtime, when RAS sunk a shot to tie the score with just eight seconds left on the clock, Burnsey immediately called a totally non-existent foul on a very bemused boy, and disallowed the basket.

When the buzzer went for the end of the last game, we ran off the court and headed straight for the school gates, trusting that all my kids would find their hosts somehow and would make it back to their homes for the evening. As we rushed past, one RAS parent did manage to ask Burnsey, "Aren't there any activities planned for the afternoon?"

"Free time at the host house," he snapped, and then added brilliantly over his shoulder as we hurried away "It's a new idea we've had to give the Tangier kids more time to really get to know their hosts."

Burnsey had located a hotel downtown where the game would be shown in the lobby. But when we emerged from the school gates, we were horrified to find that there were no taxis abroad.

This was one of the weird things about Morocco. Taxis were everywhere. In the cities, it seemed like four out of every five cars were the yellow-and-black Simcas (in Tangier) or green Peugeots (in Rabat). Any time you walked along the street or, especially, stood still on the kerbside in any city, a steady stream of empty cabs could be guaranteed to swoop towards you, flashing their lights and honking their horns annoyingly, as long as you didn't actually want a taxi at that moment. Even if you wanted a cab, but weren't in any particular hurry and didn't mind walking if you had to, you could be sure an empty one would appear instantly. But if ever you were in a panic, and *really* needed a taxi desperately because you absolutely had to get to somewhere or other, they would all suddenly vanish off the face of the earth, except for the odd one which would appear jauntily on the horizon, apparently empty and with its 'libre' light seemingly switched on, only for a ghost passenger to suddenly materialise just before it reaches you, and the driver to give you a withering glare as it swishes by.

And this was what happened now. A street normally awash with a hansom supply of cabs was now utterly bereft of them.

In desperation, we started walking towards town, even though it was a long way on a hot afternoon. We scurried along the dusty roadside under the merciless sun, dodging random holes in the ground and various unidentifiable dead creatures, casting agitated glances behind us in the hope that a taxi would appear. Eventually, a big cruiser pulled up next to us, a tinted electric window slid down, and an American voice asked us if we wanted a ride. It turned out to be one of the RAS parents, having just collected her son and his two AST hosts. We sheepishly climbed in and, deflecting all questions about what we were doing and where we were going, accepted a lift We bailed out a diplomatic distance from the hotel, and within minutes we were downing a couple of Storks and Abiding With 100,000 people at Wembley.

We decided to make things interesting by having a draw on the goalscorers. We each picked a player from each team, Newcastle and Liverpool, at random. If one of our players scored the first goal, the other guy had to pay a forfeit, with the sum decreasing with each subsequent goal. I was convinced I was onto a winner when I picked Malcolm Macdonald (a striker and total goalmachine for Newcastle) and Steve Heighway (a Liverpool winger, who didn't score very often but was at least an attacker), whilst Kenny got Frank Clark (a big lump at the back for the Geordies), and Alec Lindsay (the scouse left back who hadn't scored a goal since the War. And that was the 100 Years' War).

Predictably, our spectatorialisation was strongly tinged by these selections. I was very hopeful about Supermac, but Newcastle were mostly defending and he rarely got the ball. Heighway was getting a good bit of possession but mostly in deep positions from where he embarked on a few runs but never listened to my bellowed advice to just keep going all the way. Clark was only likely to score from a corner or a free kick, and Newcastle were so on the back foot that neither of those eventualities looked like materialising. So all Burnsey's meagre hopes rested on the shoulders of Alec Lindsay.

About twenty minutes in, with the game still scoreless and the big pot still up for grabs, Lindsay picked up the ball with a bit of space to move into. For once, it seemed like he was listening to the exhortations emanating from a hotel out in North Africa.

"Go on, son, move forward." And he did. When he was closed down, he knocked the ball in to Toshack's feet in the centre circle.

"Keep going, go on, Alec, get up there." And he did. He sprinted forward, over the halfway line and through a very high and flat Newcastle back line. Meanwhile, Toshack had laid the ball off to Case, who was facing the goal and could see Lindsay racing clear.

"GIVE IT! GIVE IT TO HIM!" screamed a near-hysterical Burnsey. And he did.

As Lindsay collected the ball and advanced on goal, the advice from two thousand miles south, although now probably loud enough that he could hear it, became so garbled and incoherent that it was unintelligible. But, incredibly, this man who hadn't scored since Pitt was the Prime Minister (and I'm talking about the Elder), and who now found himself unopposed in front of goal in the FA Cup Final, needed no advice from Kenny, and he calmly clipped the ball past the advancing keeper.

Lindsay's celebration at Wembley was understandably quite wild. But it was nothing in comparison to Burnsey's leaping, roaring tour of the lobby of the Hotel de Paris in Rabat, which also took in a detour out of the door round a couple of palm trees and an impromptu dance with a startled matron walking by in her black djellaba and veil.

Another difference between the two celebrations was that Lindsay's was cruelly brought to a quick and premature close by the sight of the raised linesman's flag over on the far side of the pitch. He had raced through a fraction too quickly, Case had delayed his pass a fraction too long, and the linesman had judged him marginally offside. Newcastle restarted with a relieved freekick, and the game resumed.

A couple of minutes later, Burnsey came back down from orbit and resumed his seat, telling me not to pay him yet because there would be more to come when Lindsay went on to complete his hat-trick. He greeted my news that the goal had been disallowed with such a withering don't-try-such-an-obvious-old-trick look that after a couple more tries I gave up trying to convince him.

It was very funny, but even I had to feel a little sympathy at the sight of his face when, eventually, about five minutes later, a caption came up on the screen reading 'LIVERPOOL 0 NEWCASTLE 0'.

After the game, a slightly richer Heath (Heighway had scored the second goal, sandwiched between two from Keegan) and a slightly chastened Burns made our way back to the flat Burns shared with his girlfriend, Fauzia.

Burnsey had explained that he had found Fauzia 'on the street' (whatever that meant). She had originally, officially, come into his flat to give her a roof over her head, but it seems that one thing led to another, as it tends to do in such situations, and she became a fixture.

They had a bit of a torrid relationship, I learned later in the year. Burnsey worked very hard to teach her English, and then managed to set her up with a secretarial position working in the US Embassy. But he told me that she was neurotically possessive and jealous.

At the end of that first school year, Burnsey came up to Tangier and stayed a night with me on his way through to a flight from Gibraltar and on eventually to a camp in New England where he worked every summer. He told me that, after agonizing for weeks, he had decided to leave Morocco and, more significantly, Fauzia.

"I've got to get away from her, Heathie," he told me. "I love her, and we are tremendously happy together almost all the time, but she has an evil paranoid streak which is so destructive. It's not good for either of us. If I don't get away now, I just know I'll be tied to her for ever, and I honestly think that, although she would never see it, it's best for her as well as me that we split up."

I knew he was serious about all this, because he had stopped humming.

"So are you going to tell her it's all over when you get back after the summer?"

Burnsey looked grim. "That would never work. You don't know how crazy she can be. If I come back to Morocco, she will never let me live on my own. She's threatened to murder me if I try to leave her, and I believe she would."

We were having dinner in a tiny, scruffy cheap Spanish restaurant in a back street round the corner from my flat, which was one of my favourite haunts.

An excellent plate of paella for two was on the table in front of us. Another strange thing about Ken Burns was that he had no appreciation for food at all. He merely ate to keep himself alive, and it didn't make any difference to him what the food tasted like. An epicure he was not. But even by his standards, he was showing absolutely no interest in the food in front of him.

"Do you know what she did? She told me about this later. The first time we made love, she saved some of my semen in a hankie. She took it to a witch doctor, and he performed some mumbo-jumbo on it which I can't even imagine, but she says that because of this, we are inextricably tied together and we can never part."

"So you're never coming back?"

"Nope."

"Have you told Fauzia?"

"Are you kidding? She's told me she will commit suicide if I leave her. I think she still might do so when she finds out, but shit, Heathie, I can't allow that kind of blackmail to ruin my life, can I?"

"Well, no, I suppose you can't. So have you told the school?"

"No. I'm going to write a letter to Fauzia as soon as I get to the States, and once she's had a chance to read that, I'll call the school and tell them I can't come back. I'll give them plenty of time to find a new guy for my job."

"So have you got all your stuff with you?"

"No. I couldn't pack too much, or Fauzia would have got suspicious. But it doesn't matter, because it's all just crap anyway. Maybe Fauzie can sell a few things and make a bit of money. I think I've done all I can for her, Heathie, don't you? She's got a good job now, she speaks English. She'll be fine. She's a hell of a lot better off than when I first met her."

Just then the phone rang. As Burnsey was talking, I watched the grizzled old patron, Francisco, come out of the kitchen and walk across to the instrument, which hung on the wall across the little room, behind where Burnsey was sitting. He spoke a little into the receiver, and then turned and looked at us. Just at that moment, my friend, who had been so involved in his own words, seemed to suddenly register that something was happening. He stopped talking suddenly, and half turned towards the old man.

"Eet's... for you," the patron said, in a hesitant and puzzled voice.

The blood drained from Burnsey's face. He suddenly took on the look of a cornered quarry, a mouse facing a cat with no possible way to escape.

With immense weariness, he pulled himself out of his chair, his eyes meeting mine for a brief second with the look of the condemned man going to the gallows, and he slowly crossed and took the phone from Francisco.

Burnsey's end of the ensuing conversation consisted of a lot of denials. "No, of course not," and lots of reassurances, "Yes, of course", and lots of, "Okay" and, "I promise" as well.

How the hell had she found him? Although the restaurant was one of my favourites, I certainly didn't eat there every night. I recalled now that the last time Burnsey and Fauzia had been up in Tangier together, we had eaten there, but that particular night, Burnsey and I could have gone to any one of half a dozen eateries. And even once she had guessed where we were, how had she found the phone number? They didn't exactly have Yellow Pages in Morocco in those days, and it was such a backstreet dive I wasn't even sure that it even had a name.

Maybe her witch doctor had helped her.

Burnsey replaced the receiver, and, his whole face and body somehow drooping, he returned, a thoroughly defeated man, to his seat. He sat with his head in his hands for a long time, silent, and I said nothing.

Finally, he lifted his head. "It was the fucking golf clubs!"

"She left for work this morning, and I was leaving right after that to get the train. At the last minute, I couldn't bear to leave my golf clubs behind, so I grabbed them. When she got home and found I'd taken them too, she knew I was leaving for good."

"But how? Surely you could be thinking of playing golf during the summer?"

"No. I'd already told her that there is nowhere to play where the camp is." He shook his head in disgust at his stupidity. "What a blunder."

"Anyway," he went on," she won't let me leave with those clubs. She's taking the night train up here, and she's going to get the clubs from me before I catch the ferry in the morning and take them back to Rabat."

"Wow! She is crazy, isn't she? And what will you do now?"

He looked up again with those trapped animal eyes, and said, "I can't leave her now, Heathie."

Over twenty years later, Burnsey is still the Athletic Director of Rabat American School. He and Fauzia are married, and they have two children who are now in college in the States.

Witless boneheads

I have a love-hate relationship with rugby.

That is to say, I hate the game: I hate the brutality, I hate the ridiculously complicated rules, I hate all the mindless wallowing in the mud, I hate the stupid shape of the ball. Most of all, I hate the macho male ethos of the game, which is still as strong as ever, despite the transparent and cosmetic attempts to mask it by introducing touch rugby and encouraging women to play. But at the same time, curiously, the word love could be used to describe my feelings about rugby. That is love in the tennis sense of the word, i.e. zero, which is precisely the amount of rugby I ever want to play, watch, or talk about.

The summer of 1966 was of course the golden moment of English football, but that was precisely the time when a gangly 11-year-old Rob Heath found his dream of one day playing for England in the World Cup Final cruelly shattered. Because my two elder brothers were such villains, and had such a terrible trouble-making reputation at the local (football-playing, by the way) grammar school, my parents decided to give me a break by sending me to the afore-mentioned (rugby-playing) public school, Ashville College.

Not only were we forced to play rugby at this barbaric institution, if you were any good, which, despite my abject refusal to tackle, I was deemed to be, purely because I was bigger and faster than most kids my age, which just goes to show what a crap sport it is, we were forced to play games against other schools on Saturday afternoons. So, during a period when Leeds United possessed the finest club team ever seen in Europe, with the possible exception of the Puskas-Di Stefano-Gento Real Madrid side of the late 50s, while they were demolishing all-comers at Elland Road, I was standing shivering miserably in a muddy field just a few miles away watching clumsy oiks scrabbling in a heap for possession of a weirdly ovoid lump of leather.

At the very moment when Mick Jones scored his fourth goal in the famous 5-1 devastation of Manchester United, for example, I was carefully stationing myself in a position where I wouldn't have to tackle some odious Neanderthal from Wakefield as he galloped through a Heath-sized gap in the Ashville defence for his fourth try.

Although I detest all rugby players, I learned early on that there are two distinct sub-species, and while one of them, the backs, are merely repugnant, the other, the forwards are the very lowest form of life on the planet, ranking clearly below cockroaches, tsetse flies, and even Manchester United fans. If Oscar Wilde did indeed eschew the pleasures of cricket because the game required a player to adopt such undignified positions, he must surely have been totally appalled by the concept of a rugby scrum. I mean can there be anything else in the world of sport, or indeed in the world of *anything*, that is so pointlessly hideous to behold, let alone to participate in?

Who invented the scrum? Surely that prize cretin, William Webb Ellis, whose jolly jape at Eton one day, picking the ball up and running with it during a game of football, is fabled to have instigated the whole rugby disaster. Why wasn't he simply put up against a wall – they're supposed to have a great wall at Eton aren't they. But hang on a minute, it wasn't Eton, it was of course Rugby, but anyway, why wasn't he summarily shot? That's what I want to know. Anyway, surely he didn't pick up the ball, run with it a bit, then put it down and say, 'I say chaps, why don't eight of you all lock arms and crouch down over there as if you're somehow taking a communal crap, and eight of us will do the same over here, and then we'll all push mightily against each other and see which side the ball comes out, what?'

The only thing worse than a scrum is a ruck.

The only redeeming feature of the ruck is that it is a godsend for the writers of dirty limericks.

The ruck has all the barbaric bestiality of the scrum, plus it is a free-for-all.

As I have already said, I was actually quite a successful player in junior rugby. I used to play in the centre or on the wing, and on the rare occasions when the witless boneheads up front used to manage to produce the ball, and on the even rarer occasions when the moron at scrumhalf elected to actually pass the ball, and on the rarer-than-the-sighting-of-an-Apollo-butterfly-in-Wigan-in-January occasions that none of the club-fingered saps inside me didn't drop the ball, i.e.

when I actually received a pass, I would pretty well score every time, from anywhere on the field.

I intimated above that this was due to my size and speed, but I have to say there were a couple of other factors. Of course, my brilliant body swerves and dazzling sidesteps helped, but the major reason why I was rarely tackled was that I was motivated by fear; a morbid fear of being caught in a ruck. If I was brought down, the thought of all those size twelve boots with no doubt sharpened studs bearing down on me from two sides like competing combine harvesters was so terrifying that I invariably rolled away from the ball and let the other side have it. But it was the dread of being tackled and then possibly piled upon by all those horrible forwards that was my main motivation as I eluded opponent after opponent en route for the tryline.

Obviously, I find the whole concept of rugby pointless and baffling, but what specially mystifies me, apart from the issue of who invented the scrum, is how the forwards can possibly get any pleasure out of the game. They have to exert vast amounts of effort pushing and shoving, scratching and biting, probably enduring random acts of sodomy as well, just to make the ball emerge so some fancy Dan whose shirt isn't even muddy can do a bit of flash running and sell a dummy or two, thereby catching the eyes of all the girls watching on the touchline. And when all that inevitably fails, just after they have picked themselves up from the muddy heap they were in, they have to lumber off after the ball to go through the whole excruciatingly aimless exercise all over again.

And the most ridiculous thing about the whole game of rugby is that, when all that sordid grappling and aimless tearing up and down the field is over, and after the referee has delivered dozens of full-length lectures on the laws of the game to the players in the middle of the contest (you wonder why the players don't take a notebook and pencil on the field with them)... when it is all over, the team with the best footballer in their ranks is invariably the winner! The entire object of the game is to run the ball over the other team's line and score a try, but the deciding factor always comes down to which team has the best kicker.

Anyway, the day I walked out of the gates of that school for the final time, I was thrilled, for many reasons, but one of which was that I would never have to play rugby ever again. So when, many years later, Pierre Laurent, my counterpart at the Lycée Française in Tangier, suddenly materialised at school and asked me if I wanted to play in a rugby sevens tournament, I didn't waste any time weighing up the options before responding with a scoffingly chuckled, 'No, thanks'.

But I was too hasty, for as I listened more to Laurent it turned out that he was offering me a free trip to Portugal for the weekend.

Apparently, a group of teachers from various schools in the city traditionally entered a team in the annual Algarve Sevens tournament. The team bore the imaginative title of Tangier Teachers. They were due to fly out to Portugal that very evening, but one player had suddenly found that he could not travel. (He couldn't find his passport!) His ticket and hotel room were already paid for, and rather than see it go to waste, they were desperately seeking someone to take his place.

This, as I said to Laurent, was a totally different kettle of poissons. He had no idea what I meant, but as soon as school finished I raced home, threw some kit into a bag, grabbed my passport, and caught a cab to the airport.

In the departure lounge, I discovered that the other lads in the team were a fine bunch, and I could see that an excellent weekend lay ahead of me. They were of course keen to know how much of a rugger bugger I was, to which I replied that I had only played a little bit a long time ago at school, but I foolishly couldn't resist saying that I had been pretty good. I stressed, though, that it had been a very long time since I had played any rugby at all, and felt confident that I would not be used in the games except in emergencies. Although looking at the size and, especially, the shape of several of the squad, I did worry that emergencies might occur distressingly frequently.

As we checked in at the hotel in Portugal, we were greeted by a representative of the organising committee, who gave us all the information about the tournament. The other lads were extremely perturbed to learn that we were in a group with The Borderers. These were apparently a crack outfit comprising the top players from the Scottish border clubs like Hawick, Jedburgh etc. They had won this competition for the past five years, and we were due to play them in the opening game on the stadium pitch in the morning. There was much petrified gnashing of teeth over drinks and dinner that night, and I went to bed feeling very sorry for the lads who would have to face these superhuman Scots on the morrow.

Nevertheless, I breezed down to breakfast feeling very pleased with myself; delighted to be tucking into a splendid buffet on a terrace overlooking a wide sweep of

Atlantic beach. Then the bombshell struck; in an act of inconceivable folly, the selection committee had decided to start *me* on the wing against The Borderers.

The scrambled egg turned to ashes in my mouth. I stuttered and smiled nervously, thinking and hoping that it must be a particularly weak attempt at rugby team humour. But no, the fools were deadly serious. My hasty reminders that I had not played for decades fell on deaf ears as they explained their not very brilliant logic that what we needed above all in a game like this was pace and fitness, and since I was the youngest member of the squad, I was an obvious selection. Not only that, but apparently I was due to mark a 19-year-old who just a week before had played for Scotland B against the touring All Blacks!

I felt very queasy on the drive to the ground, only managing a few forced smiles in response to the banter which was still flying around. All the team seemed remarkably light-hearted, considering the ordeal we were about to face. Although I did note that it was the ones who weren't starting who were the light-heartedest. I was concentrating on my gloomy deliberations on the likely quality of the Algarvian hospital facilities. As we got changed, though, and I pulled the famous red and gold quartered jersey on for the first time, I felt my unease gradually metamorphosing into a steely determination.

These brave lads, who I barely knew, had given me this free trip to Portugal, and now had offered me this fantastic opportunity to play in a top-class game at a stadium in front of a big crowd of people. I resolved that the least I could do was to give it my all, as long as my 'all' didn't involve making or receiving any tackles. I tried to remember all the things I had learned, the things that had brought me success, back in the days when I did play rugby.

In particular, I had been a very clever defender, adept at anticipating the flow of the game enabling me to usually manage to be in a position where I didn't have to make a tackle. This skill usually worked well, although when one is playing outside centre, and the opposition outside centre waltzes through unopposed for a try while one is temporarily on the opposite wing, one does have to expect a little tetchiness from one's teammates.

That's another thing I hate about rugby: the ridiculous system whereby a team that has just conceded a try has to line up on their line whilst the opposition attempt a conversion. It is a situation where sniping and finger pointing is inevitable, and even the most robust of team spirits is bound to take a hammering.

What worried me at this point was that my cleverness at managing to always be in the wrong place at the right time might not work so well in the vast open spaces of a 7-a-side contest, and I would be exposed as the pusillanimous coward that I was.

We ran out onto the pitch, and tried to do two things: act as if we were a proper team, and not look at the Scots. We failed in both endeavours. A little bit of stretching was successfully carried out, but all attempts at the most simple passing and a bit of coordinated movement resulted in embarrassing fumbles and misunderstandings. While we were doing this, our eyes were magnetically drawn to the blue shirted paragons of athleticism and/or brawn who were gliding about at the other end of the pitch with arrogant confidence. I immediately picked out my likely opponent. He was about six foot, with the legs of a sprinter and the upper body of a middleweight boxer.

Neither the earthquake nor the tsunami that I had hoped for intervened at this stage, and all too soon we were huddling before the kick-off. Pierre managed to say, "Let's give these bastards a surprise and hit them hard," with a straight face, and the game kicked off.

As the very first game, and the showpiece opening of The Borderers' defence of their title, there was a big crowd in the stadium. All the other teams were present, along with most of their supporters, plus a fair sprinkling of rugby fans, either locals or holidaymakers. After all, there were some quality teams in the tournament – not only The Borderers, but teams from Australia, South Africa and France. Oh, and Morocco.

One part of the razzamatazz for the tournament was a commentary broadcast to all the spectators on the stadium pitch. And this is how the commentary went for the opening of the Borderers v Tangier Teachers match:

"And so The Borderers open their defence of the trophy as they kick-off to the Teachers... and that's a good take... oh, but the Teachers have lost the ball, and here goes McTavish... and it's a try for The Borderers with just six seconds on the clock! Surely that must be a World Record for a team kicking off!"

We had caught the ball cleanly from the kick-off, but it was immediately smuggled from the holder at the first tackle, at which point it seemed like our whole team were adopting my studiously-run-into-a-position-where-you-won't-have-to-tackle strategy, and Jock (probably) McTavish (apparently) had an unopposed run to the line.

As a team, to a man, we were angry and humiliated. We all burned with a furious inner desire to violently respond. But leaving the pitch, cuffing the smartarse commentator round the head, and stamping on his microphone, were just not viable options at that moment, for we still had hordes of Picts and Scots attacking us.

From the next kick-off, we did manage to offer a little resistance and make a bit of ground before Pierre, who was our only half decent player, executed a reasonable grub kick into touch to take us into their half of the pitch. Their backs lined up at an incredibly steep angle, and my opponent was a long way away from me. Nevertheless, I subjected him to the meanest, toughest glare I could muster. Even though the glare was totally wasted, because he wasn't looking anywhere near me. I thought, "I must be at least five years older than him, and that's got to be an advantage. He's only a big kid."

Surprisingly (not), they won the ball from the lineout, and as they started to spin it out along their backline, I set off sprinting full pelt at the young winger. "Hit the kid hard as soon as he gets the ball," I was telling myself, "and maybe he won't be so cocky." When he did receive the ball, I was only a couple of steps from him, and I launched myself at him with a rush of adrenalin, determined for once in my life to make a solid, crunching tackle.

Effortlessly, he danced to one side, leaving me sprawling on the ground, and took off for the line. I had barely picked myself up before he crossed for their second try, much to the delight of our friend the commentator.

It ended up 73-0.

Not such a bad score, really, although I suppose I should point out that we were only playing ten minute halves. My rival only scored three of their eleven tries, but I'm afraid I can't really take any credit for that because it was purely because the blokes inside him usually broke through and scored themselves long before they needed to pass to him. I distinguished myself, however, by valiantly chasing after every player who broke through, earning quite a few cheers for my pluckiness from the spectators, none of whom were aware that I was pretending to be running back at full speed but was in fact timing my effort perfectly so that I would always arrive just too late to make a tackle. I didn't touch the ball once.

After a break to lick our nurses and bruise our wounds, we took the field again to face the Porto Pirates. They were much more like our kind of team, consisting of a mix of Portuguese (enthusiastic, but not really knowing the game) and expats (mostly slightly past their sell by date). We fancied our chances against this lot. We had rotated our squad, and all the lucky bastards who had missed the Battle of Bannockburn were drafted in. I was left out, a decision about which I was ninety per cent relieved and ten percent outraged.

We kicked off, and Pierre sent the ball deep. As they ran it out, the ball was fumbled forward and a knock-on was called. Extraordinarily, we somehow won the scrum, the ball was thrown back to Pierre, and he proceeded to drop a magnificent goal from a good forty yards out! Yes! 3-0!

But they turned out to actually be quite a well-drilled team, and we were soon behind. The lads really showed heart and character, but we eventually went down 24-3.

That brought us to our crucial final group game against The Sorcerers. These were a curious bunch who were out on tour from Devon or somewhere. They were a shabby outfit who had also shipped over fifty points against The Borderers (who had played their second string) and had lost pretty soundly to the Pirates as well. Heath was back in the side, and we really thought we were in with a chance of beating this lot and thus avoiding last place in our group.

I didn't fully understand how these rugger chaps organised their tournaments, but it seemed that you qualified for a different level of knockout play on the second day, in descending order of quality, each time you lost. The Cup was the top prize, and apparently we were already out of contention for that, and the plate, but if we won this one we could have a go tomorrow for the soup tureen. If we lost, the best we could hope for would be a slotted spoon. Or something like that.

It was a great game. We played our best rugby of the day, but they also played much better than we expected. I actually got into it a bit, getting the ball a few times, even making a few good runs, and not shirking too many tackles. They led early on, we fought back. It was close at halftime, we came desperately close to taking the lead, but they defended stoutly and broke away at the end to score and win 12-6.

Agony. Gutted. But I had actually enjoyed it.

We dragged our exhausted bodies back to the hotel where, after showers and short power naps, we convened at the poolside dining room to feed our monstrous appetites and relive the glories of the day. Every minor triumph on the pitch was elevated to heroic status, and we were soon convinced that we were definitely the strongest team in the Butter Dish competition. After a good few drinks, some of us ended up in the water, from where I decided to give a synchronized swimming performance, even though I lacked the minor requirement of a partner to synchronize with. As I attempted to execute a sort of leaping pirouette, the effort required for my right leg to kick hard against the resistance of the water, after all its exertions during the day, proved just too much, and my hamstring twanged.

So the next day, I was confined to limping around on the touchline, the Tangier Teachers were deprived of the services of their dashing young winger, and, no doubt because of that, they lost all three games and finished last in the Eggcup Tournament.

As we wearily bade each other farewell back at Tangier airport, and climbed into taxis to take us to our various homes, we reflected on a weekend of tremendous laughs even if we didn't meet with much success on the pitch.

And I wondered if I was the first person ever to come home from a rugby tournament with a synchronized swimming injury.

The merest whiff of rodent

As I have already intimated, public relations were absolutely paramount at AST. For McAllister, nothing particularly mattered so long as the two big public set piece occasions of the year – the play and graduation – were spectacular successes.

The same year that *Lord of the Flies* was such a disaster, though, graduation also threatened to go horribly rugby ball.

The problem derived from the fact that the previous year, McAllister had deviated fatally from his normal policy. Rather than choose a senior to play the lead role of Prospero in *The Tempest*, he had chosen a junior, Frank Worthington. Having had his fill of poor Frank when the following year's play came around, he had overlooked him for the part of Jack, offering him instead the less-than-thrilling role of the ship's captain who walks on stage at the very end of the play and rescues the boys. Not surprisingly, Frank turned this part down, and instead spent the year quietly, and indeed frequently not quietly, simmering in resentment at the way Aidan Butterworth had usurped his position, not only as star of the play, but also as Headmaster's 'favourite'.

Throughout the year, Frank, who lived in the dorm as a boarder, was a major disciplinary problem for all the teachers. But as the end of the year loomed, word somehow got to McAllister that Frank was planning to publicly denounce him at the graduation ceremony.

I learned during my tenure at AST that the job of Athletic Director required me not only to organise various sporting activities and teach PE; I was also called upon by Gary to undergo any task that required strength, speed or athleticism in even the slightest measure. So, when he decided to kidnap Frank Worthington, I was the obvious candidate to play the heavy.

I was summoned to his office one morning and told to go to Frank's room in the dorm, pack all his things, and then hide his suitcase in the boot of the school car. That done, I was to collect the unsuspecting lad from class, and bring him to the front of school, where McAllister informed him that his father had called from their home in the Lebanon to say that there was an urgent problem with his passport. He was to go with us in the school car immediately to the American Consulate, where they would sort everything out.

The boy hesitated at first. It seemed plausible enough, but I think nevertheless he detected the merest whiff of rodent somewhere. With a little bit more time to think, he might have asked why it was necessary for Mr. Heath to go with them on a simple trip to the consulate, and indeed why I was sitting in the back of the car with him. But as a student, even a recalcitrant little git like him, he was basically programmed to believe what teachers told him. He got into the car, McAllister took the wheel, and we set off.

If there were any doubts in his mind about this trip, he definitely started to entertain real suspicions when we reached the roundabout at the top of the hill, and turned left along the airport road, rather than right into town. I knew he suspected there was something a little fishy when he immediately shouted "Hey! This isn't the way to the consulate! Where are you taking me, you fucking assholes?"

He ignored my lame response that we were taking a new route to avoid traffic, and, realising exactly where we were going and why, opened his door and tried to jump out. This might have been a smart move if it wasn't for the fact that Gary was doing 70 mph by this point. I grabbed him around the waist, pulled him back in, and managed with some difficulty to subdue the writhing maniac in a headlock with one arm, and reach across and pull the door closed with the other. McAllister sped on without a moment's hesitation, blithely oblivious to the muffled curses and flailing limbs behind him.

I was beginning to wonder how we were going to handle the airport bit, but I should have known that Gary would have it covered. He eschewed the airport car park, and pulled up instead right outside the main door of the check-in hall, where we were met, to the astonishment of both Frank and myself, by two armed policemen. I knew Gary had friends in high places, but even he must have concocted a good story this time. They frogmarched the by now subdued young kidnapee straight through into a small VIP room next to the departure lounge, whilst McAllister gave me a ticket and Frank's passport and told me to go and check him in for the flight to Beirut, and then join him in the bar.

Gary bought me a well-earned drink, and we sat nervously watching the airport going about its business. McAllister had timed it very well, though, and we did not have long to wait before they called the passengers to board the Beirut flight.

One thing I did see from my vantage point at the bar was the TAP man in Tangier. His name was Rui Marques, and I knew him quite well, because he had a son, Carlos (no doubt named in a fit of revolutionary zeal) at our school. Carlos was one of the players in my school team. He was a great kid who really loved his football, and I found out why one night when I was invited to his family home for dinner; his father was a football fanatic. He was a big Sporting Lisbon fan, but he had an impressive knowledge of world football, and we talked long into the night about the game.

But he also told me a very funny story about his job at the airport. He said that he had noticed that some of the other airlines were starting to use walkie-talkie systems so that the office in the airport could communicate more quickly with the personnel organising take-off. He thought this looked efficient and also projected an excellent image of the airline, so he wrote to his head office in Lisbon asking to be issued a set. A couple of weeks later, he received a box containing one walkie-talkie, along with a note saying that they couldn't afford to buy him a full system just now, but they had found this odd one lying around and he might be able to use it.

So, despite the tension of our situation, I chuckled to myself when I saw Rui crossing the passenger hall, stopping, unclipping his set from his belt, issuing a terse instruction, and then striding off in a different direction.

I noticed that he had acted out this little charade right in the middle of the hall, in the most highly visible spot available.

A few minutes later, we watched all the other passengers begin to file out of the door and walk across the tarmac to climb the steps to the plane. When everybody else was on board, Frank emerged from his little cubby, still flanked by the two policemen. He seemed to be subdued and resigned to his fate now, walking with his head bowed and a guard holding each arm. As McAllister went across to give him his passport and boarding pass, though, he suddenly tried to break away. He managed to yank one arm free, but the other guard was alert enough to hold on and force his arm up behind his back.

"Help!" he yelled. "I'm being kidnapped! This man is a filthy pederast!" And he spat in McAllister's face.

The only people in the airport at that time, apart from all the officials and airline employees, were a pod of British tourists waiting for a flight to Luton. I think one woman glanced up from her Catherine Cookson book for a brief moment, but apart from that Frank's frantic cries were totally ignored. I don't know whether it was traditional British reluctance to get involved with any foreign monkey business, or whether they had already seen and heard so many bizarre things during their two weeks in Morocco that one more just didn't register anymore, but, to our huge relief, Frank's attempt to draw their attention to his plight was a total failure.

He was dragged, still struggling, across the tarmac and up the steps, and a few minutes later Gary and I, from our positions in the bar, saw the plane racing along the runway and climbing into the air. I couldn't be sure at that distance, but I thought I could just make out a passenger at one of the windows, pounding on the glass and mouthing the words "You bastards! I'll be back!"

If Gary noticed that, he showed no sign of it. As soon as he saw the plane safely up and banking over the Straits heading east, he turned to me, raised his glass, and said, "Well done, Rob. That's the last we'll see of that little asshole!"

But he was wrong, because as soon as Frank's Dad found out what had happened, he and his son got on the next plane back. With his lawyer. By the following lunchtime, the Worthingtons were holed up in the Hotel du Rif, and Gary was shut away in his office with the legal eagle.

All the time I was there, we were always told that AST was teetering on the edge of financial meltdown. The dormitory, which had been built just a few years previously, and was supposed to secure the school's financial future by attracting loads of the expatriate oil kids who were not allowed by law to stay in Saudi Arabia after the age of fourteen, was splendid, and almost empty. It was even emptier now that Frank Worthington had gone. Yet McAllister must have put together some pretty substantial compensation package, because by the end of that day it became known that the Worthingtons had gone for good, and young Frank had signed an undertaking never to return to Tangier and probably, just like Yossarian at the end of *Catch-22*, to always say nice things about Gary McAllister and the American School of Tangier. (Even if he appeared on CNN or something.)

At the graduation ceremony, the little children sang beautifully, some Korean kid played a flute, and Gary

McAllister handed papyrus rolls to sixteen proud seniors, reserving a special hug for Aidan Butterworth. It was a charming ceremony, but I wasn't the only one to notice the presence of two very large men in bulky suits on either side of the door, and several of us couldn't resist the urge to keep glancing nervously over our shoulders throughout the festivities. But Frank Worthington remained merely a ghostly presence, felt, but not physically seen.

An even more outrageous jaunt

One day, I found a letter in my box at school which contained an invitation to enter my girls' basketball team into a tournament in Gibraltar. Not only that, but the Rabat American School were also invited. It sounded like a tremendous opportunity for high-jinks.

AST had about as much money budgeted for athletic trips as Alec Lindsay had Cup Final goals in his career, but I managed to strip the costs down to a bare minimum by booking us into a very cheap and basic hostel, and enough girls managed to persuade their parents to stump up, for the trip to be on. It would have been even cheaper if we could have taken the ferry, but McAllister, in a rare moment of concern for academic progress at the school, decreed that we couldn't take the extra day off which that would entail, so we had to fly out on the Friday night. Burnsey's girls came up by bus overnight on Thursday and took the ferry Friday morning.

When we met to get on the bus for the airport, one girl, Nadia, told me she had not been feeling well all day. But she looked okay to me, and knowing how hard she had worked for the tournament, and how excited she was, it didn't even occur to me that she shouldn't come.

As it happened, she had a very virulent and contagious bug. I had always tried to drill into all my players the importance of passing, and Nadia did me proud; she passed that bug onto every other player on the team.

By the time we landed in Gibraltar, Nadia was running a huge fever and had the energy level of a rag doll, whilst a couple of other girls were complaining of feeling weak and lacking appetite. It seemed this was one of those forty-eight hour flu jobbies, and for the whole weekend after that I had three fluid groups of players: those who were starting to get sick, those who were sick as dogs, and those who were on the mend.

Somehow, by juggling the (relatively) healthy players as much as I could, we managed to fulfil all our fixtures in the tournament, although predictably we had even less success than we would have done with a fully fit team.

The crunch game for us, of course, was against RAS. They were the team we always wanted to beat. I wasn't optimistic about our chances at the best of times, because Burnsey was a good coach who really worked hard with his basketball teams. Now that we had the influenza factor, I felt we had very little chance. I did contemplate having my girls sit behind the Rabat bench during a previous game, breathing hard at Burnsey's players, but this was such a nasty little illness that I couldn't wish it upon anyone.

Trying to marshal my depleted resources before the game, I hit on a good plan. I took all the girls' temperatures, and the five with the lowest ones got to start the game. Then during the game, I had the girls on the bench constantly taking each other's temperatures, and if any player dropped below 99, I bunged her on. Halfway through the first half, I had to call a time-out because it was time for three of the players on court to take their medicines.

We lost, but under the circumstances, I thought we did well.

The only good thing about this sickness was that the poor girls were all so ill and drained by the end of each day that supervising them in the hostel, which I had expected to be a nightmare, proved to be a doddle. All they wanted to do was sleep, and my hardest task was keeping track of when they were supposed to be taking their medicines.

Burnsey's mob were also staying at the hostel, but in a different building to ours. He did not have it so easy, but on the last night he came knocking on my door after midnight and said, "Hummmm-comeon Heathie, mmmm. I've finally-hmmmm-got them all hmmm quiet. Let's go hmmm out for a dri-hmmmm-nk." I wasn't sure we ought to leave twenty-one girls on their own, unsupervised and unprotected in the middle of the night in a foreign country, but Kenny insisted it would be alright as long as we only went for a swift one or two.

We stumbled back into the building after 2.30 a.m., considerably the worse for wear. We had found a very sleazy little dive and the gins we had consumed had, we were just beginning to realize, been very sub-standard. The way my stomach was spinning and my head churning, or vice versa, I could believe that they had mixed neat gin with anti-freeze or white spirit or something.

After throwing up, then checking that all the girls were safe and sound, then throwing up again, I just had enough about me to set my alarm and then I passed out.

We had to be up at the unfeasible hour of 4.45 in order to make the walk (thankfully very short, our hostel was located right next to the airport) across the runway to the terminal building for a 6.15 a.m. flight. It was already well past three when I set the alarm, it was dead on 4.35 a.m. when I slept right through the alarm, and it was well after five when I woke to a pounding on my door.

I leaped out of my bed in a panic, and opened the door. Two of my kids stood there. "What time are we supposed to be at the airport?"

By some miraculous process, I managed to get ten girls out of bed, dressed (these are teenage girls we are talking about!) and chased across the tarmac and into the airport just in time for us to still check-in for the Tangier flight. All that with a pounding head and extremely wobbly innards.

The plane which hops from Gibraltar over to Tangier obviously does not need to climb very high. It has got to be one of the most spectacular flights in the world, right from the heart-stopping take-off. The runway, which we had scuttled across just a few minutes before, is placed on the only piece of flat land inside the Gib-Spain border, across the narrow isthmus between the rock and the mainland. It is not a wide isthmus, and as a result, the runway is not very long. The pilot taxis to the very end of it, then opens the throttle, sending the plane careering apparently straight towards the water. At seemingly the very last second, the nose lifts and you're up in the air. Immediately, though, the plane banks left to avoid the cliffs on the far side of the Bay of Algeciras. If you're sitting on the left side of the aircraft, there is a terrifying moment when the wing dips towards the water, the tip seeming to skim across the top of the waves, and you feel sure you're going to slide into the bay.

As the plane rights itself, passengers are given a glorious view of the two rocky sentinels at the Eastern end of the strait. Gibraltar derives its name from the original Arabic name of Tarek's mountain, or Jibr-el-Tarek, and directly opposite on the African side is its counterpart, the other Pillar of Hercules which provides such a magnificent natural portal to the Mediterranean, Jibr-el-Moussa.

Because they create such a natural funnel between two huge bodies of water, and between two massive chunks of land, the Straits of Gibraltar are not surprisingly renowned for their amazing swirling currents, and also for their strong and capricious winds. As the little plane ploughs up the middle of the blue strip of water, offering more marvellous vistas of the rocky cliffs and sandy coves on both coasts, it is buffeted and battered by these powerful and unpredictable winds.

So, as I said, a spectacular flight. But also an invariably bumpy one, and in my extremely ropey condition it was the bumpiness rather than the spectacular which I noticed.

Fortunately, I was able to blame my World Championship vomiting performance, as much as I could communicate anything, through teeth more gritted than the approaches to Edinburgh Castle on a cold January night, on the dreaded lurgy which the girls had all suffered from. They were all very understanding, neglecting to point out that none of the other sufferers had experienced the symptom of serial vomiting. They managed to organize themselves as far as passports, luggage, etc. went. A school bus was there to meet us, and I lay on the floor groaning whilst it toured the city dropping my charges off.

It was a very pathetic creature which eventually crawled gratefully into my bed and slept for fourteen hours.

A month later, Burnsey was on the blower with a proposal for an even more outrageous jaunt.

A good friend of his was the AD at an American School in London, and it seemed they were hosting a big football tournament for schools from all over Europe. One team had dropped out, and Burnsey's pal had invited him to enter a squad in their stead. Ken Burns was a lot luckier than I when it came to financing things, because the Crown Prince of Morocco was one of his students, and the young heir loved sports and was in the habit of paying for any extras Burnsey asked him for. Moulay Rachid, the prince, was not allowed to join this particular junket, due to security concerns, but he was nevertheless prepared to fund the thing. Nevertheless, Burnsey was concerned that he didn't have enough reasonable players to compete at the elevated level of the London tournament, so he was proposing a joint RAS-AST team, combining our best players.

When I asked Gary McAllister for permission to take six boys out of class for a week to play football in London, he had a tricky decision to make, balancing the boys' academic wellbeing against the life experience of travelling to another continent. I could see he was teetering on the edge, and could have come down either way (None of the lads, to be honest, were pulling up any trees with their grades, and it's true they could ill afford to miss any class time), so I mentioned the fact that this was a very prestigious tournament, and our participation would bring great kudos to the school.

I booked the flights that afternoon.

At such short notice, the best flights we could get were with Air France, with a stopover in Paris. We had a tough time organizing visas for the few kids who needed them at such short notice. Burns had to leave one kid, a Somali, behind because he never got his visa, whilst my Ahmed Mettawa, who had some kind of weird stateless status, although he was actually Libyan, came along armed only with a 'Laissez-passer' issued by the Egyptian government. That caused plenty of frissons on arrival in London, but eventually, they let him in.

And then there was Tarek Burr.

Tarek had dual nationality. He turned up at the airport with his French passport, but left his Moroccan one, which contained his visa for England, at home. We had no choice but to dispatch him in a taxi to fetch it, but he never made it back in time, and we took off without him.

We had already resigned ourselves to the fact that our squad would be one player short when, at our hotel in London, a fax arrived, informing me that Mr Burr would be arriving at Heathrow at midnight. I took the tube out to the airport, but when I got there, I saw that there were no flights from Paris arriving around that time. The whole thing seemed like a wild goose chase. I was just trying to figure out how long I would have to wait there before I could justifiably get back to the hotel when, dead on midnight, a sliding door hissed open and Tarek came wandering through it.

I never knew how he had got there. I certainly didn't believe the fantastic story he told me. He said that when he'd got back to the airport, he had been put on a plane to Rome. After four hours in Rome airport, they had told him to take an Austrian Air flight to Geneva. But once in the air, he had realized that the plane was going directly to Vienna. He claimed that the plane had landed specially at Geneva, just to drop him off, and from there he'd picked up a Swiss Air plane to London.

The kids, of course, were absolutely ripped at the idea of getting a week off school, travelling to London, and playing football as well. However, they were less ecstatic about the whole affair when we had to literally shove them out of the changing room and onto the pitch to play their opening game against the American School of The Hague.

It was 9.00 a.m. on a cold November day in England! We were expecting lads who were used to playing on dusty pitches in roasting sunshine to go out and perform in a chilling, sleety gale on a rutted surface with a swathe of half-frozen mud right up the middle of the pitch.

They really didn't fancy it. They stood around in a semi-catatonic state during the 'warm-up', and no amount of coaxing or cajoling from Burnsey or me had any effect.

Our keeper, a big, strapping, but volatile and somewhat brittle American boy from RAS called Kyle, looked particularly unimpressed. Which was pathetic really, because he hailed from New England, where the winters are much worse than anything you might get in London, but I guess he'd been softened up by years in sub-tropical Africa.

I don't suppose our short-sleeved shirts helped much. Most of the players had at least two long-sleeved shirts underneath (and some even wore sweatshirts), making them look more like penguins than footballers.

Burns and I, the coaching dream team, were less than optimistic as the game kicked off. We'd lined them up in a conventional 4-4-2, but they had independently adopted their own curious formation which seemed to consist of several fullbacks, several wingers, a few wide strikers, and virtually nobody anywhere in the middle of the park. Like wildebeest, they had all naturally migrated to the small grassy areas near the touchlines, abandoning the icy, muddy part of the pitch.

As a coach, I really like my players to think for themselves, take decisions on the pitch, and not just be automatons following orders from the side; but I must admit, this particular outbreak of lateral thinking on the part of our players was not welcome. My frantic exhortations, and the total apoplexy of my coaching partner, failed to have anything more than a minimal effect. Luckily, ASH were crap. Despite playing the whole game virtually unopposed, they only managed to get five shots on target the whole game. We lost 6-0. The other goal came when Kyle took a short goal kick, and when the ball was passed back to him, which was allowed in those days, he declined to pick it up (possibly anticipating the rule change, but more likely not wanting to get his gloves damp). He tried to trap it, and it bobbled over his boot for an own goal. Kyle walked off at the end without a drop of mud on his knees or his jersey.

We had four hours to lift the boys and somehow motivate them to bounce back from such a morale-sapping defeat before the now-vital clash with Munich International School. We told the kids to enjoy the warm showers, and then we sat them down in the warmth of the clubhouse, and left them to ponder the situation while we went down the pub.

Things looked brighter in the afternoon. The wind had eased, the sleet had stopped, and although none of the kids agreed, Ken and I thought the weather was quite pleasant. The players were warmed, fed, and rested. But we had a daunting task. Munich had drawn 0-0 with The Hague, so our situation was clear-cut; we had to win to go through to the knockout stage.

We could tell straight away in the warm up that our team were finally here to play; Kyle actually dived to save a shot! The game itself was a fascinating dual between two totally contrasting football cultures. The Morocco All-stars tried to get the ball down on the ground, pass it around, and run at defenders. They were skilful, but lightweight and perhaps, okay definitely, over-elaborate. The Munich players were larger, stronger, quicker and fitter, and their game consisted of launching the ball goalwards from every corner of the pitch.

Both defences looked terribly vulnerable: we couldn't deal with all the high balls played into our box, and their defenders were terrified by opponents who dribbled at them or executed one-twos. But nervous finishing and good goalkeeping kept the score goalless until the stroke of half-time, when our centre half (one of the RAS players, incidentally) fatally misjudged yet another hoof up the middle, saw it bounce over his head, and their striker nipped in to score.

Our hopes looked grim as the second half ticked away. Even when Lamarti equalized with fifteen minutes to go, dribbling calmly round the keeper after leaving the defence flat-footed with a simple exchange of passes, we still needed another goal.

The last minutes rushed by, and Burns and I were desperately looking at our watches when we won a corner. As we piled everybody forward, the ball arced into the box, and was met by a defensive header out to Tarek Burr, standing a yard or so outside the area. There were probably eighteen or nineteen players between him and the goal. The keeper was off his line, having made a sortie to reach the cross but not got near it. And the kid who had slept the night on my hotel room floor after a tour of the airports of Europe and, he claimed, virtually hijacking a plane, calmly took the ball on his chest and then, as it dropped, lobbed it with the side of his foot high over everyone's head, but just inches under the bar, for a brilliant winning goal!

Even some of the kids agreed with us that the weather the next morning, as we prepared to face the defending champions, the American School of Paris, in the knock-out phase, was almost pleasant. A low sun shone from an unfeasibly blue sky, albeit with no real warmth, and the wind remained mercifully light.

ASP were a good side; they had all the brawn and size of the Munich team, but they could also play a bit. But we were clearly getting acclimatised now, both to the conditions and to each other, because of course, these lads had never played together as a unit before. Whilst they were definitely dominant, we played some good stuff and were certainly not overwhelmed.

It was a tense and very exciting match, which remained goalless right up until the closing minutes. Right at the death, we thought we had won it when good old Lamarti repeated the one-two and again got in behind the defence. This time, instead of dribbling the ball in, he tried to slide the ball under the keeper's dive. The keeper just got a piece of the ball, and as it rolled agonizingly towards the line, a defender appeared from nowhere and slid in to hack it away.

So, it was penalties.

I think subjecting adolescents to the peculiarly cruel torment of a penalty shootout is a terrible thing. But it wasn't my tournament, and I was in no position to change anything. I won't catalogue the awful emotional turmoil which got us there, but it ended up 3-3 after the regulation five penalties, and we moved into sudden death.

Ken and I looked at the miserable, exhausted, terrified bunch of players we still had at our disposal to take a penalty.

"Right," I said brightly, "who wants to take the next pen?"

Most of them were trembling in fear and trying to hide behind each other, desperately hoping not to be asked. The two players who had already missed were already being treated for depression and anxiety attacks by a crack team of psychiatrists over on the touchline, whilst their parents back in Rabat (note, they were both Burnsey's players) were removing all sharp objects from their houses and fitting protective padding to the walls of their rooms.

Ken Burns had a brainwave. We still had one player eligible to shoot who was absolutely brimming with confidence. Kyle! He had already saved two pennos. I may have intimated earlier that he was a bit of an up and down character, but right then he was quite definitely UP. When Burnsey suggested him, I turned round from my position in the centre circle to have a look at him. Paris were due to shoot first in the sudden death, and while their coach was also trying to decide which poor kid to subject to such medieval torture, Kyle was pacing around the goalmouth, slamming his gloves together, and roaring "Come on!" and "Bring it on!" in the intimidatory way only an American can.

I knew Burnsey was right.

We called Kyle over, and told him that he was going to take the next kick.

"Yeah!" he bellowed.

He ran back to his line, smacking his gloves together again. (I tried to dismiss the thought that he reminded me of Batman.)

ASP finally selected their sacrificial victim, and the poor wretch set off, his knees wobbling, on the longest walk in football. I would have bet my house that he was going to miss, but luckily there were no bookies available, especially since I didn't even have a house, because he tucked a confident shot neatly just inside the post.

Kyle, though, had read his intentions, dived the right way, even got his fingertips to the ball, but he couldn't keep it out. He leaped to his feet and let out a roar of frustration. Then, as the ASP goalie took his place between the posts and the ref replaced the ball on the spot, Kyle marched to the edge of the box, ripping off his gloves as he did so and hurling them furiously to the ground, turned without a moment's hesitation and rushed at the ball, taking a massive, angry swipe at it with his right foot, designed to send both ball and keeper, if the latter were foolish enough to get in the way, right through the back of the net.

But he didn't quite connect the way he had hoped to. In fact, the furious swing of his foot only made the most minimal contact with the ball, enough to send it spinning wildly on its axis but to move merely a couple of feet towards the goal before coming to an embarrassing halt.

Paris went on to retain their trophy. We stayed till the end, watching the final with a wistful feeling that we could easily have been there ourselves. Kyle had a bit of a down phase after the penalty shootout, but by the end of the day he was up again. Burnsey told me that he was a Mormon, and it was his faith which kept him going, which explained a lot.

On our last morning, we had several hours to play with before we had to get out to Heathrow, and we decided to let the kids have a look around the city. The host school had put a bus at our disposal, and we asked the driver to drop us at some convenient central location, and to return to pick us up at midday. He decided that the corner of Hyde Park, just near Marble Arch, would be the best place, and duly delivered us there.

Once we got off the bus, I shepherded the kids into the park to get away from the noise of the traffic, gathered them around, and delivered a stern lecture about security and about exactly what they could and could not do. Then I told them they had to be back by 11.50 a.m. because the bus could not wait there for anyone, and set them loose.

During this process, I had been vaguely aware of a greyish bloke in a shabby coat who was loitering on the fringe of our group, almost as if he was trying to listen in to what I was saying. When the kids had gone, and Ken and I were starting to debate which pub to go to, this guy materialized next to me and said diffidently in a thick Eastern European accent, "Excuse me. Arrre you a speakerr?"

I looked at him in utter mystification, but then Burnsey started to laugh. "Don't you realize where we are?"

I was instantly assailed by the image of this poor downtrodden soul, risking his life to get out of Poland or East Germany, struggling his way across the continent and the channel, all to fulfil his life's dream of visiting Speakers' Corner, and seeing for himself the very crucible of free speech and democratic values. And I could imagine the letter he would scrawl in his spidery hand to the shivering wretches cowering back home under the communist yoke:

Dear Gregor,

The political debates are lively and radical–why only today, I heard a rabble-rouser exhorting a group of young people to keep their hands on their wallets, and to keep out of sex shops. This was obviously a metaphor for...

Despite our misgivings, the kids were all back on time, and we boarded the bus for the drive along the Westway to the airport.

Burnsey was not looking forward to the return journey, because, since we had had to book our flights so late, we had had no choice but to opt for an itinerary that involved a seven hour layover at Charles de Gaulle airport. None of the kids had visas for France, so they had to stay in the airport. Ken and I, of course, being British, did not need visas. So we had decided that one of us should stay at the airport to supervise the fifteen bored and unruly teenagers, whilst the other could go off into Paris and enjoy a meal, a movie, and maybe some Beaujolais Nouveau.

In a moment of downtime at the tournament, we had run our own little one-on-one sudden death penalty shootout to decide who should occupy which role. Burns had hit the post with his first shot, and I had smacked mine triumphantly up the middle as he dived hopelessly to his left.

After careful deliberation, meticulously weighing up the pros and cons, I informed the whining Ken, who was pathetically trying to claim that we had said it would be best-of-three, that I was going to plump for the high-life-in-the-city option. I hastened to explain to him that my choice had nothing to do with my personal desires, and that in fact my main motivation was what was best for the kids. He was clearly so much more experienced than I at maintaining order, because the RAS kids were so badly behaved compared to the angels we had at AST.

There was one minor fly, however, wriggling about annoyingly in the smooth, pristine ointment. That fly was called Vladimir.

Vladimir was the son of the Yugoslavian ambassador to Morocco, and as such was the possessor of a diplomatic passport, and so he was just as free to travel into Paris as was I. His father had requested that Vladimir be allowed to go into the city during the stopover to visit some relative who lived there, and Burns, the cretin, had given him permission.

I was damned if I was going to babysit a hunk of seventeen-year-old Slovenian, though, so I showed him where to get the airport bus and then left to get the metro into town.

A spot of lunch at Chartier's... a film at the Gaumont... an inordinately expensive grand café crème on the Champs d'Elysee as the beautiful people sauntered by. What a wonderfully civilised city Paris is.

I had read that it is said that if you sit for long enough at the Café de la Paix outside the Opera, eventually the whole world will pass by, so, worried that they might all be waiting for me, I made my way across there so they could all cross me off their list.

But all too soon, it was time to make my way back to the airport.

When I got there, I found. for some reason, a rather frazzled Burns waiting for me at the checkpoint for the gate. He had already got the kids and himself through, but he suggested that I should wait a bit because Vladimir had not yet returned.

I sat down with my book where I could keep an eye on the gate and see when the great lump arrived. As the departure time grew nearer, and he had still not appeared, I started to hear announcements on the tannoy requesting, "Monsieur 'eath and Monsieur Turcinov to proceed to gate twenty-three immediately."

Eventually, I felt constrained to present myself to the Air France people at the gate, and explain what was happening.

"You are Monsieur 'eath? Alors, you must go through immediately!"

I explained patiently that I couldn't do that yet, because I was a teacher and I had to wait for my student, who would no doubt be there at any minute. Burnsey, on the other side of the checkpoint, tried to explain the same thing, which only confused matters.

Ignoring the increasingly agitated chatter of the French, he and I discussed across the gate what we should do.

"You'll just have to wait there till he comes," said Ken.

"But what if he never turns up?"

"I don't know... you'll just have to find him somehow. Here, take this," and he passed an envelope across to me.

"What is it?"

"Two thousand dollars. Emergency money. The school gave it to me before I left, in case anything went wrong."

I was starting to think this wasn't turning out that badly, but he saw my eyes glinting and called sternly "Get receipts!" over his shoulder as he was physically manhandled off down the walkway by a steward. Frogmarched by a Frenchman, now there's an indignity.

Immediately, the frogmarcher was back insisting that I now hand over my boarding pass and board as well. When I refused, he said "Very well. We cannot wait any longer. We shall leave without you." And he pulled the door to the walkway closed behind him and locked it from the inside.

Two minutes later, he was back, in the company of a man I took to be the chief steward.

"Monsieur, your suitcase is on this flight, so for security reasons, you must board the plane as well."

After hearing me repeat my insistence that I could not board without my student, he turned and locked the walkway door again. But before he left, I heard him tell the people at the gate, in French, "Lock him in a room and don't let him out until the plane has landed safely in Morocco!"

Two more minutes later, an even higher Air France official arrived. The chief steward had evidently been over-ruled.

"Monsieur, if you refuse to board, you will have to go into the hold and remove your suitcase. Come with me."

"But how will I find it?" This was a jumbo jet we were talking about. I was being led through a security door and down some stairs out onto the tarmac under the plane. "Anyway, my student's suitcase is on the plane too."

"Yes, you'll have to remove that as well."

"But how on earth will I know which is his?"

"You will just have to find it some'ow."

By now, they were opening the hold, and I caught a glimpse of hundreds of suitcases stacked in containers. The whole enterprise was patently absurd. I looked up to the sky in frustration... and saw, up on the walkway just about to board the plane, the oafishly grinning figure of Vladimir.

When I got on board, I had to pull Burns off Vladimir. He seemed to be about to throttle him, and I couldn't let that happen. I wanted to throttle him!

He said the traffic had been worse than his uncle had expected.

Light-headed silliness

I used to snootily deride those at university who took drugs as lowlife wasters, and when I got to Morocco I had the same attitude. For a while.

But one day, it occurred to me that all these people must be giggling about something, and, like your classic teenager giving in to peer pressure, I jumped in to the drug cesspit with both feet.

It took me a while because the first few sessions I joined in with involved smoking hashish, and as a non-smoker I did not possess the skill base necessary to ingest the stuff. After much spluttering, I could very easily have abandoned the whole project and returned to my former position of disdainful abstinence. But eventually, enough of the fumes managed to make it into my system, and I started to experience the light-headed silliness and relaxed feeling of wellbeing which it's supposed to be all about.

Thereafter, I was quite a consistent user of the stuff. The hashish in Morocco really is tremendously good. Being a neophyte, I could not compare it with any other product, but friends assured me that it was smoother, more powerful, and less side-effecty than anything available elsewhere in the world. Plus, it was very cheap, as long as you didn't pay the tourist prices.

The cheapest place of all was in Rachid's bar.

Rachid was a wonderful guy who was a big friend of Gary and the school. He owned a splendid little bar/restaurant called The Nautilus, and AST teachers were always made extremely welcome there. They had a fantastic asparagus & cheese dish as a starter, which I could never resist ordering at least once when I was in there. As AST teachers, we were allowed to order whatever took our fancy and sign the bill at the end. One of the barmen, Mohamed or Farid, would carefully file the bill in a box at the end of the bar, and it was expected that we would settle up, at least some of the balance, every few weeks or so. This system made it a very popular place near the end of the month.

The other great thing about Rachid's was that, if you ordered your drink and then went to sit in the back room, Mohamed or Farid would bring it through with a big fat joint on the tray.

I managed to keep my consumption and behaviour under a reasonable amount of control most of the time, except one Friday night when 1st Grade teacher Boston Bill and I went over to the flat of another teacher, Micky Bates. He told us that he had acquired a jar of hash jam which he had heard was very good stuff, and we decided to give it a go and then head over to the Italian Club for dinner.

We were supposed to put the jam on toast or something, but we thought bollocks to that and we each took a couple of spoonfuls of the stuff and sucked it straight down. Bates said that he'd been told that it worked better if the stomach was warm, so we brewed a pot of tea and drank that.

Then we sat around.

Nothing seemed to be happening, so we roundly abused Bates for being so stupid as to fall for such an obvious con, scoffed at the amount of money he had squandered, took another spoonful each just in case, and set off for dinner.

The Italian Club was a wonderful institution. They had two clay tennis courts, a state-of-the-art bocce pitch, and a fantastic restaurant which we could eat at even though we weren't members. It was run by a large and extremely voluble woman called Anna, who was reputedly a former Romanov princess who had fled the Russian revolution as an infant. She was one of those remarkable people who knew your name from the very first time she met you, and always managed to give the impression that you were a special person in her life.

She produced an excellent set meal – the same every night, spaghetti Pomodoro rustled up in a vast pot, followed by a thin slice of meat with chips–and the restaurant was always packed. Although the meal was remarkably cheap, the clientele usually consisted of all the great and good of Tangier society (plus the odd AST teacher.)

That night, Princess Anna greeted us as usual like her favourite customers, and we threaded our way between several occupied tables to one over by the window that was free. We ordered a glass of wine each, and soon three plates of steaming spaghetti were served.

Somewhere around that time, I started to feel a little odd.

People on the periphery of my field of vision seemed to be making strange movements, but when I looked at them, they were sitting perfectly normally. Sudden quite alarming bangs and crashes sounded, but when I turned to look, nothing seemed to have happened. The process of eating my spaghetti seemed to be terribly difficult, and also completely absurd. I found I had to sit very still and concentrate immensely on each little step of the process, and the entire concept of wrapping the strands around my fork seemed to be so ludicrous that I wanted to burst into laughter. The strong feeling began to grow that everyone else in the room was watching me, and could see that I was really struggling.

Bill Gurney said something to me, but I could not make out the words. Nevertheless, it was clear to me that he could see I was having a hard time getting my food to my mouth, and he was trying to distract me and make me look even more stupid in front of all the people who surely really were now staring at me. But I was not going to fall for that. Making a mental note to get him back as soon as we left the restaurant, I ignored his words (whatever they were) completely, and kept my focus locked firmly on my plate.

Bates suddenly tipped back in his chair, landed flat on his back, and lay motionless.

I was surprised to see what happened next. Gurney, who told me later that he thought Bates was having an epileptic seizure and was about to swallow his tongue, jumped to his feet and started to take off the belt which held his trousers up. He was planning to somehow use the belt to hook onto Mick's jaw to keep it open (I don't know where Gurney took his first aid course), but fortunately Mick staggered back up and resumed his seat.

I now had the dual problem of concentrating on my spaghetti-eating conundrum, and at the same time stopping myself from laughing at the image of Bates prone on the floor and Gurney standing over him, apparently removing his trousers, in front of the cream of Tangier society.

I started to feel a little ill, and realized that I desperately needed fresh air. But the path I would have to take to get to the door required me to weave in and out of four or five closely packed tables; a task which somehow seemed completely beyond the realms of anything possible.

For a few more minutes, I sat, trying to keep as still as possible, staring fixedly at my plate. All the noises of a crowded restaurant now seemed to echo and take on a terrifying dimension; the clatter of knives on plates, the murmur of polite conversation, the occasional burst of laughter.

I finally felt that I absolutely *had* to make a move, to essay the terrifyingly daunting obstacle course to the door, for if I didn't do it there and then something awful, probably involving Gurney standing over me and removing his trousers, would happen.

Carefully, I raised myself to a standing position. My chair tipped back and fell over, making an alarming crash. One of the two bastards I was with said something to me, but I knew they were trying to trick me, so I ignored it. Now that I had moved my head, the whole room seemed to be slowly revolving, but in different

128

directions, in the most alarming manner. I took a deep breath, and concentrating furiously and avoiding the traitorous hand of Bates, who tried to pull me back, obviously in an attempt to bring me down in front of all those people, I somehow managed to lurch and veer in and out, around the seated people, and stagger out past the princess and her steaming cauldron of spaghetti into the fresh air.

Taking deep draughts of it, I sat on a wall, held my head in my hands, and shut my eyes. Unfortunately, even the blackness was still rotating, but at least I was not in view of all those people anymore, and so there was less chance that they would call the police and have me arrested. Keeping my eyes firmly closed, I carefully swung myself round and lay on my back, but that seemed to make the revolutions worse, so I staggered back to a sitting position.

The fresh air eventually began to take effect. I wasn't sure if I had thrown up or not, but thought I might have done, because I was starting to feel a little bit better, and I thought it might be safe to open my eyes. On doing so, I found that the wall I was sitting on was right outside the long picture window of the restaurant, and that I was in full view of all the people in there.

I was convinced now that everybody was talking about me. I imagined them complaining to the princess, asking who I was and writing outraged letters to McAllister, finding out my address and sending the drug squad round. Blackballed from the Italian Club... fired from my job... arrested!

Then I saw that Gurney, with a huge grin on his face as if he was tremendously enjoying the spectacle I was putting on, was beckoning to me to come back inside and rejoin their table. Was he mad? Did he not realize that I had already fulfilled one impossible task by getting myself out of that fucking room before I passed out, and even though I now felt a bit better, the idea of trying to get all the way past those people and back to the table without falling over or stumbling into someone's spaghetti was totally and utterly preposterous!

It occurred to me that he knew it was an impossible thing to do, but he was trying to make me do it because he *wanted* me to suffer some disastrous embarrassment, probably to try and distract everybody from his own trouser-dropping indiscretion.

"You're not catching me that easily, you son of a bitch!" I mouthed at him through the window, and I turned and set off on a weaving walk out of the gate, wondering as I did whether I really had only mouthed that, or whether I had actually shouted it.

My only aim now was to get home, and to lie on my bed and wait for the swirling in my head to die down.

I was not so far gone that I didn't know where I was, and I knew that the route home was simply to walk up the little lane leading from the club and turn right, then quickly right again onto the Avenue des Mimosas. This was my street, although I had quite a long walk up the hill, across the main road that led down from the mountain, and down the other side.

Even though, on my arrival, I had been given all manner of dire advice from old-timers about how careful I must be at night in such a dangerous city as Tangier, I had actually never felt in the least bit apprehensive, or suffered any nasty moments. But that night, all those warnings came flooding back to me. I was sure that knife-wielding muggers were everywhere, just watching for a *nisrani*, a foreigner, who was a bit worse for wear and therefore vulnerable. I became convinced that walking with a natural gait in a straight line was, at that moment, a matter of life and death. Unfortunately, in the condition I was in, it was also yet another simple thing that I now found immensely hard to do.

Nevertheless, I managed to make it up the long slope to the crossroads at the top, glaring with hostile suspicion at the few people I saw. I stopped at the edge of the main road, and looked left and right. What I saw filled me with awe. Pairs of white and red lights were advancing and receding. The pattern they made was quite beautiful. But then a growing horror gripped me; I knew these lights were very important, and that they represented something very dangerous to me, but I couldn't remember what they signified. Worse still, I knew they represented some kind of puzzle, which I had to solve if I were to get across the road, but I couldn't even recall what the nature of the puzzle was, let alone how to crack it.

I stood there for a long time, looking one way and then the other, trying desperately to remember how to do this thing. After an intense effort, I figured out two things: that I had to wait for a gap, and that the lights were moving. But I couldn't decipher which direction they were moving in, or at what speed.

I was terrified to take a step onto the road. But I was equally terrified to stay still, certain as I was that too much hesitation would alert the knife-wielding muggers to my vulnerability, so I took a deep breath and plunged across. I expected death from the unknown force of the lights at every step, but, surely due only to great fortune, I made it to the other side.

Now all that remained was a short walk down to my ground floor flat at the bottom of the hill by the roundabout. But on that last leg, a new fear assailed me. I remembered that I had a massive problem with the key to my door.

I wasn't sure why, but sometimes my key would turn in the lock of the outer door of my building first time, but other times it would stick. When it stuck, I would extricate it, and then try again; and it would eventually turn. But it might take two tries, three tries, or a hundred and four tries. There seemed to be no logic to it – I had a notion that it was something to do with different types of metal of which the key and the lock consisted, and variations in their rate of expansion–but whatever the reason, it was hugely annoying to get home and then take ten minutes or more to get into the bloody building.

Irksome and frustrating though this problem normally was, it now loomed in my drug-warped mind as the most grave life or death situation I had yet faced in this suddenly oh-so-hazardous world. The sight of someone fumbling at the door of a building would surely draw every k-w m in Tangier within minutes.

Strangely, parts of my mind were still functioning normally, and I recalled perfectly my theory about why the key did not always work. I knew that the key – ha! – factor, if I was right, was the relative temperatures of the metal of the key, and the metal of the lock. So I pulled the key from my pocket and held it tightly in my hand in an effort to warm it up... until it occurred to me that I didn't know if it didn't work when it was too warm, or when it was too cold, so then I started waving it around in the night air, hoping to cool it down.

With my heart pounding, I approached the door, fearfully glancing back over my shoulder. Just as I arrived, my neighbour from across the hall opened the door, and with a cheery "Bonsoir, Robert", held it open for me to enter. I just managed to stop myself falling at his feet to thank him for saving my life.

Inside my flat, I had enough presence of mind to carefully double-lock the door from the inside, and then I stumbled into the bedroom, and collapsed onto the bed, relief that I had survived the most perilous journey flooding over me.

As I lay on my back, the room now shifted and swirled around me almost worse than ever, whether my eyes were open or closed. I felt as though there was nothing to be done except to wait for the merciful release of sleep. Soon enough, my eyelids started to droop, and the kaleidoscopic movements began to morph into weird dreams.

But the paranoid madness this evil drug had induced in me was not about to let me escape so easily. I somehow started to believe that sleep meant death; that if I allowed myself to drift off, I would never wake up.

So now I lay in a terrible turmoil in that dark room, sweating and writhing as I fought to stay awake.

And then the madness took an even more devilish twist, as I found my mind suddenly split in a horrible schizophrenia. I didn't hear voices, but rather I felt two distinct entities fighting for control of my very being.

As I still struggled to prevent myself from falling asleep, convinced that doing so was keeping me alive, I became aware not of a voice, but of a realisation – the understanding that in fact I really did need to sleep, that sleep was the only thing that could save me from going permanently insane, and that it was some kind of demon of the drug that had invaded my mind and was trying to force me to fight sleep to give it more time to take over my brain for ever. But no sooner had I had that thought, than the opposite struck me – that the real demon that had invaded my head was trying to persuade me to go to sleep so it could kill me once my resistance was down.

I don't know how long I lay on that bed, gripped by an utter madness that at the time was totally real. I was by now utterly terrified; nowhere in my consciousness was there any more even the vestige of an awareness that this was just the effect of a drug I had taken. I felt that I truly had been invaded, occupied, by an utterly evil presence, but I felt powerless to fight it because I was incapable of distinguishing between it and my true self, because it disguised itself as my saviour and set me against myself.

I was mad.

When I looked back on those minutes or hours, much later, I didn't think to myself, "That's what madness must be like." I thought, "That's what madness *is*."

I *was* mad. It was a truly terrible experience.

At some point, though, I must have finally drifted off into a troubled sleep in which I only had a nightmare that I was mad.

Meanwhile, Gurney and Bates had managed to finish their meal without further mishap, all trousers remaining respectably up, and had set off for home. Worried about what had happened to me, good old Boston Bill took a detour past my flat. He rang my bell, but I think the ringing barely penetrated my convoluted dreams, probably manifesting itself as a phone call from the devil.

He knew where my bedroom was, and guessing accurately, from my lack of response to the bell, that I was passed out on my bed, he walked round to my bedroom window and pounded on it, calling out "Heath! Are you okay?"

This commotion jerked me out of my sleep. I recognised the voice, and the paranoia was evidently still active because I was instantly filled with the conviction that Gurney had plotted my entire descent into madness for some evil purpose of his own, and had now come round to finish me off. I leaped from my bed to the window and yelled with all the ferocity I could muster, "Fuck off, you bastard!"

I took it easier on the hashish after that.

Rocks, stones and lumps of concrete

One Saturday lunchtime, I threw my boots, jockstrap and *War and Peace* into a bag and walked to the Café des Sports where I met up with my chums from the RST team. We sat around drinking coffee for a while. The banter was in Arabic, none of which I understood, and French, some of which I should theoretically have understood, but, in truth, none of which I really followed either. Only two players, the teenagers Driss and Karim, made the effort to talk slowly to me, and they soon lost patience with my stumbling responses.

Presently, we all boarded a bus and set off on the four hour drive south to the bubbling metropolis of Sidi Slimane. I sat on my own, and alternately dozed and watched the passing scenery. Arabic pop music played as we curved around and over the bridge over the river and passed the castellated village of Asilah, with the Atlantic Ocean glittering bluely behind.

I recalled the magnificent day the previous month when three of us had got up really early on a Saturday morning, meeting up at the bus station down by the port.

Even at that hour, several buses were preparing to depart. Passengers shoved to get on board and grab the best seats, whilst incredibly lithe young boys scrambled all over the sides and roof, belying their skinny limbs as they hoisted all manner of goods and chattels up and secured them with filthy ropes. A man stood in front of each bus, yelling the destination, and we joined the battle to get aboard one described as "CASA, CASA, CASABLANCA!"

Eventually, when the driver felt the bus was as full as it was going to get, he slammed it into gear and, choking the crowds left behind in a foul belch of thick diesel smoke, headed out of the depot, along the corniche road next to the magnificent sandy bay, and finally turned right and threaded through the suburbs and out onto the main road south.

But when he got to the great river south of Tangier, before the road swept inland to the new bridge, we called him to halt, and jumped down. We then picked our way across the old bridge, barely standing after a destructive surge several years earlier, crossed a few hundred yards of scrub, and emerged onto a glorious Atlantic beach.

It was still quite early, but the sun was climbing into the sky. We set off on the 14 km walk south in the sand, the heat slowly building, but a wonderful breeze pushing in over the pounding surf to keep us comfortable. Only the odd fisherman ("Salaam Alaikum"), did we meet in all those hours, sitting by their boat occupied with their nets, usually with a dog who growled at us protectively, but we saw gulls wheeling overhead, flocks of sanderlings working the shoreline and occasionally exploding into flight as we drew too near. Every now and then, one of us would spot a few flying fish, and once, some dolphins arching out of the water, quite close in.

Gradually, we made out a speck on the horizon at the end of this dead straight beach, and it grew and grew until finally, pleasantly hot and tired, we climbed up through the ancient castle walls of the little town of Asilah. In the centre of the village were several restaurants, with tables set out on the pavement. We chose one and sat with our Storks while the patron threw dozens of freshly caught sardines onto the grill. After our exertion, the anticipation caused by that classic aroma was almost too exquisite, and the fish, when they arrived, were heavenly.

After a long, splendid and simple lunch, we took a bus back to Tangier.

On that later Saturday, after Asilah the RST bus paralleled the coast all the way to Sidi Slimane, but we caught nary another sight of the Atlantic.

On arrival we checked into a thoroughly adequate hotel, and there ensued many hours of sitting around playing cards (the other players) and reading *War and Peace* (me.) During one of the even more idle than usual moments, I noticed that there were seventeen players with us, which, given that the squad size for a Moroccan league game was sixteen, meant that one of us would have made this entire riveting trip for nothing (apart, of course, from the riveting). I didn't waste a lot of time speculating on the identity of the gooseberry.

After a very tasty tajine dinner, I decided to take a late evening stroll around the streets, and sample the sights and delights of Sidi Slimane. Ten minutes later, I was in St Petersburg and Andrei was enjoying an intoxicating dance with the glamorous young Natasha Rostova.

Sure enough, the following day when we assembled in the hotel for our team talk, the Bulgarian blockhead confirmed that it was I who would not be pulling on the famous green shirt. When we got to the ground, I was sent up to sit in the one stand that ran the length of the touchline, whilst the others changed. I sat there glumly, annoyed with myself for not having brought my book, thinking about Pierre Bezukhov and how ridiculous were the Freemasons. Eventually, the teams emerged in dribs and drabs from the changing rooms, and started warming up, whilst the previously almost empty stand began to fill a little with Sidi Slimanians.

Suddenly, I heard someone say, "Hello, Mr Heath," and I was astonished to see El Habsi approaching me. I didn't even know that he was an RST fan, but he insisted that he was a real diehard and that he had hitch-hiked down from Tangier that morning to watch the game. It was a huge relief to have someone to talk to, and El Habsi confirmed that he was indeed a very knowledgeable fan by sympathizing with my plight and naming at least three players who I should have been starting in place of.

By the time the game started, there were probably a couple of hundred fans dotted around the stand. El Habsi and I seemed to attract no attention, even though the presence of a *nisrani* at a Moroccan Second Division game can't have been a very common occurrence.

The game itself was a scrappy and dull affair. We had no Rubio in our line-up that day, due to an injury, and neither side possessed a player with the skill or guile to get hold of the ball in the middle of an admittedly very bumpy and hard pitch and play a bit of creative football. El Habsi (the creep) and I agreed that it was a scandal that the only player with that class and ability was sitting in the stand. The only times the interest level increased just a little above comatose was when our giant centre-forward Hassan went anywhere near the ball, at which point whistles and curses erupted from our cohabitants in the stand.

El Habsi informed me that this was because Hassan was from Sidi Slimane, and had left the club a couple of years previously in search of glory with the big boys of RST. A Bigtime Charlie is of course never popular when he returns to his roots, but it has to be said that Hassan was certainly not doing anything to endear himself to his former acolytes. Despite the fact that he was a big, strong lad, he was crumpling to the ground theatrically at every challenge from the centre-half. The ire of the locals was exacerbated by the fact that the ref was falling for the dives just as much as Hassan was falling to the floor, although, perhaps fortunately, my green-shirted teammates managed to waste every free kick quite spectacularly.

Deep into the second half, the game appeared to be meandering aimlessly towards an inevitably barren conclusion. But with about ten minutes to go, the poor maligned Sidi Slimane centre-half finally lost it, and we got some entertainment at last. After being penalized yet again for a totally innocuous challenge, the lad could not take it anymore and gave the ref a right tongue-lashing. The bastard-in-black responded predictably by booking him.

This was just more than the defender could take, and he lost control completely. Only the restraining efforts of his colleagues prevented him from physically attacking the ref, and a good old melee, of which I noticed Hassan carefully stayed well clear, ensued for a while. Passions were also running high in the stand, and we tried to make ourselves as inconspicuous as possible. Finally, everything seemed to have calmed down, and the game resumed with yet another Tangier free kick. However, as luck would have it, the ball quickly ended up quite close to the ref, and the still seething centre-half saw his chance. Obviously making only a minimal attempt to pretend to be going after the ball, he sprinted across and barged into the ref, knocking him to the ground and then – exhibiting the good old as-well-be-hung-for-a-sheep-as-for-a-lamb philosophy – trampling on him a bit for good measure.

This predictably produced huge cheers from the stands, but also, inevitably, once the ref got to his feet, the expulsion of his assailant. Now completely out of control, he produced a splendid performance on his way off, first kicking a bucket of water halfway across the pitch, then demolishing a wooden chair which was by the touchline before finally stomping off down the tunnel to huge cheers from the locals.

As the final few minutes of the game played out, El Habsi nudged me and whispered that I should take a look at our fellow spectators. They were all scouring the stand for rocks, stones and lumps of concrete. But if things were looking ugly, they were incredibly about to get even worse.

In the very last minute, RST finally managed to play a decent pass into the box. Hassan moved onto the ball and then, with the most blatant dive even he had done, sprawled to the ground. No one was surprised when the ref awarded us a penalty and, just in case there was perhaps one local fan who had not yet reached a pitch of murderous apoplexy, Hassan dusted himself down and then dispatched it himself.

The situation was exacerbated by the geography of the stadium. The tunnel emerged from under the middle of the stand, which meant that all the players and officials had to leave the pitch and pass right under the livid and now armed mob of Slimanites. As soon as Hassan's shot hit the back of the net, the ref blew for full time and then legged it for the tunnel, where he and his colleagues passed through without harm under the protection, surprisingly considering his outrageously biased performance, of the home team players. The Renaissance players, on the other hand, all congregated on the far side of the pitch from the tunnel, where they simply stood in a fearful group eyeing up the fans in the stand. A few of the mob tried a potshot at the team with a smaller stone, but most of them were obviously saving their ammunition. There were a few policemen around, but they amazingly showed absolutely no inclination to do anything to protect the beleaguered players.

After a brief standoff, my teammates evidently decided that there was no option but to run the proverbial gauntlet. The police were showing no signs of helping them, and the fans were equally showing no signs of losing patience and dispersing; so, on a word from one of them, they ran in a tight group across the pitch and with their hands held pathetically above their ducked heads they scrambled down the tunnel. And they made it relatively unscathed, because Hassan foolishly chickened out of the rush and stayed where he was, leaving himself totally isolated and exposed, and most of the fans, noticing this, still held their fire.

Several minutes passed, with Hassan standing hesitantly on his own and the local lads jeering at him and taunting him. Eventually, the policemen decided that they had better do something, so they grudgingly walked over and, very bravely actually, provided the hated cheat and turncoat with a human shield which managed to scuttle to safety down the tunnel under a hail of rocks and concrete lumps.

And that left El Habsi and I alone in the stand with a couple of hundred bloodthirsty Sidi Slimonians. Neither of us were in any doubt that if they realized there were two Tangerines in their midst, we would very soon be marmalade, but luckily, as we tried hard to shout and act as angrily as everybody else in the hope of blending in, the entire mob raced up the terraces and vanished down the central exit.

We waited a few minutes to allow them all to get well away from the stadium, and then went down under the stand to join the team in the changing room; except we found instead that the entire mass of murderous maniacs had not left the stadium at all but were besieging the away changing room. The players were barricaded inside, and the angry horde was seething outside, pounding on the door and yelling, "Death to Hassan!", "String 'em Up", etc., or so I guessed, and even though I spoke no Arabic I don't think I was far wrong.

What to do?

One option might have been for El Habsi to tap a few of the chaps on the shoulder and say, "Excuse us. This is a non-playing member of the Tangier team. Could you just let us through?"

Seems an obvious solution now, looking back, but for some reason, it didn't occur to us at the time. Instead, we decided to just leave the stadium and try to find our own way on foot back to the team hotel.

We climbed some steps and emerged onto a wide area of waste land which surrounded the stadium, only to find that the authorities had finally decided to respond to the burgeoning civil unrest, and a row of riot police were advancing across the space between us and the exit, each holding a length of wood which I didn't think they were going to use as walking sticks.

We were in a predicament.

Behind us, the devil of a riotous mob, in front the deep blue sea of menacing stick-wielders. Relatively new to Morocco as I was, I knew enough to know that these guys were highly likely to be from the whack-on-the-head-first-and-ask-questions-later school of riot police.

We were saved by El Habsi's quick thinking and actions. He spotted a jeep at the far end of the line of stickmen, moving with them at walking pace, and saw that if we were quick we could just about get to the jeep before the line got to us. "Come on!" he yelled, and set off at a sprint across the open space at an angle. Guessing his intent, I hared after him. We did indeed reach the jeep ahead of the advancing police, and El Habsi breathlessly shouted what I assumed was the briefest summary of our situation to the officer.

There was a horrible pause. The jeep was still moving, as was the line, and we were skipping backwards just a few feet from the men who I dared not look at but I sensed almost had their sticks raised ready to crash them down on our heads at a word from their commander. He seemed to have an air of arrogance and indifference, and I was convinced he was just going to shrug his shoulders and look away, which I am sure would have been enough to seal our fate, but then to our huge relief, he gestured for us to get up into the jeep with him.

After that, the situation was resolved surprisingly swiftly. The rioters dispersed instantly once they saw that the stickmen were on the scene. As far as I could see, there was no serious head-bashing; just a few skirmishes and the odd glancing blow with a stick just to gee people up a bit. The team were escorted onto their bus, but the officer who had saved us insisted on giving us a lift in his jeep back to the hotel where we arrived just as my nervous teammates were alighting, much to their surprise. El Habsi was quite rightly hailed as a hero by all and sundry, and was immediately offered a lift back to Tangier on the team bus and, to finish this little tale in true Enid Blyton style, it was a very tired, relieved and happy bunch who set off on the road north out of Sidi Slimane well past midnight.

That game at Sidi Slimane was the first intimation for me that everything in Moroccan football in those days was not quite completely above board. No doubt if I was more tuned in to the changing room banter I would have picked up on this before. As it was, I had learned that *dahal* meant 'cross', but I never noticed any talk of *double-dahal*.

It was also the beginning of the end for my own career with RST. I had wasted almost an entire weekend and been bored cardboard for long periods of time; I had narrowly escaped from a very threatening incident; and all for a game the result of which had apparently been stitched up before we even left home.

It wasn't long after that trip that I started to miss the odd training session. It was bloody hard work training at the hottest time of the day, and always stressful trying to get a taxi back from the stadium in time for my afternoon class. I was asking myself what was the point when Monsieur Buggeroff apparently had me behind one-eyed Hamid, the hunchbacked stadium dogsbody, in the pecking order for team selection. Before long I just quit going altogether, and it was significant that nobody came round begging me to return.

Nevertheless, I continued to follow the fortunes of the team. The board of RST were desperate to get back into the top division, and all season long we were vying with Oujda, a team from way out east on the Algerian border, for the Championship and the one promotion spot that went with it. As luck would have it, our final game of the season was at home to Oujda, and we went into the game level on points but with an inferior goal difference. This meant that an RST win would see us Champions, but a draw or loss would hand the crown to Oujda.

On the morning of the game, a bright, clear spring Sunday, I took a long walk up onto the mountain and ended up at a café near the stadium. I loved this place because it had magnificent views over the Straits of Gibraltar, but it also faced slightly west and you could see how the straits opened out into the Atlantic Ocean. I liked to ponder the fact that I was smack bang on the top left hand corner of Africa, at Cap Spartel, and it was possible to stand at just the right angle so that I could imagine the ocean stretching out before me for thousands of miles, and the land stretching out behind me for thousands of miles.

This particular day was phenomenally clear. All the time I was in Tangier I was fascinated by the way that sometimes Spain was not visible, there were other days when you could just make out something on the horizon, and then some fabulous days when it was so close you could make out every detail of the cliffs and you almost felt you could swim across. But on that amazing day, from that wonderful spot, I could see all along the coast as far as Gibraltar, and I could see way up the coast on the other side, all the way to Cadiz. The sea was a gloriously deep, sparkling blue, and a delicious warm but fresh breeze blew in off the Atlantic.

As I walked in, I bumped into Rubio and a few other players who were just leaving to go up to the stadium. They greeted me with great warmth, and invited me to come with them to the ground. But I knew that would entail loads of the sitting around doing nothing which was the main reason I'd quit the team, so I declined. Instead, I sat for a couple of hours reading a week-old *Daily Telegraph* and sipping mint tea whilst I luxuriated in the view.

Finally, I walked across to the stadium, past astonishing numbers of policemen, and paid at the turnstile to go in, anticipating some real fireworks as the top two teams in the Moroccan Second Division slugged it out for the title in front of a rare full house of 20,000 excited Tangerines.

What I saw was the most anodyne 0-0 draw ever. Each team, as soon as they got possession, simply passed it around in little triangles in the middle of the park, making no effort to get anywhere, whilst the opponents equally made no effort to get the ball back. Every now and then, someone would try a ridiculously optimistic shot from about forty yards out which would either fly high or wide or would dribble through to the keeper.

The crowd, so excited leading up to the kick-off, progressed in mood rapidly from feverish support of the boys in green, through a shocked and disappointed silence at how badly they were playing, to a fierce rat-smelling realisation that there had to be an ulterior explanation for such a performance. Oujda were playing as one might expect a team needing just a point for the title to play, keeping the ball when they got it, and sitting back as soon as they lost it. But RST, needing a win, should have been pressing the ball, swarming all over their opponents when they had the ball, and much more direct and ambitious in possession.

By the second half, even the derisive whistles died out as the game inched drearily towards its apparently inevitable conclusion. A lot of the fans drifted, disillusioned, to the exit, pausing to hurl one final curse at their erstwhile heroes before departing. Only a few thousand were left to witness the bizarre scenes which followed the final whistle.

One would have expected the Oujda players to have celebrated jubilantly on the field as soon as the point they needed was secured, but in fact the instant the whistle blew, they all ran in unison to the bench area. Seeing them coming, a man in a suit leaped out of the Tangier dugout and raced for the tunnel. Incredibly, the man was carrying a suitcase! He didn't get very far before the Oujda players caught up with him, and there ensued a massive tussle in the centre circle for possession of the suitcase.

All this was just too much for the remaining fans on the terraces. All the policemen I had seen outside the ground before the kick-off were now inside and lining the track all around the pitch. The disgruntled fans, livid to see such obviously dodgy goings-on displayed in front of them in such a brazen manner, began to throw things. Since all the players were too far away in the middle of the pitch, it was the police who became the targets of the bottles, stones and, I was now beginning to learn, what are the staple ammunition of your average Moroccan football hooligan, lumps of concrete picked off the crumbling terraces.

A high-ranking officer, sporting a splendid uniform replete with all the stars and stripes, walked across the pitch to appeal to the fans to stop, and I was very amused to see that when they not only refused but actually concentrated their aim on him. he started to pick missiles up from around his feet and throw them back at the crowd!

So distracted was I by these shenanigans, I had lost track of the events on the pitch, and when I looked back, I saw everybody going off down the tunnel, and I did not know who had ended up with the suitcase. The rioting was also dying down, and it seemed like all the fun was over, so I made my way home, trying to figure out what had happened and why.

Later that night, I finally hit on an explanation which I thought fitted the events I had witnessed. The key element was an incident that happened just a few minutes before the end of the game; thinking back, I recalled that after eighty-seven minutes of pussyfooting around, a pass had suddenly been made by an RST player in behind the back four for Rubio who was suddenly free down the right. He had taken it clear and then pulled it back for Hassan to direct a great header at goal, but the Oujda keeper had made a superb save. The whole incident was completely out of character with the rest of the game.

My belief was that the Oujda team had offered the Tangerines a suitcase full of cash if they agreed not to try to win; RST had accepted the bribe and played throughout as if they were trying not to score, but their plan was to double-dahal Oujda by getting a late goal, and still keep the cash. Only the brilliance of the visiting keeper had foiled the plan. After their failed attempt to score, though, the Oujda players realized RST had tried to shaft them, so they determined to try to get the suitcase full of cash back as soon as the game was over.

In the months that followed, I occasionally ran into a couple of the players, but if I asked them about that game and the mysterious suitcase, they suddenly had a really hard time understanding my French.

Ee, it's a funny old game, is football.

The heady excitement of having a real house

The first flat I lived in was a mistake.

After two weeks hitching and sleeping in a tent, followed by a nasty knife threat when I took a room on my first night, I was very keen to get a flat of my own. So when Hamid, the school business manager, took me round to a few potential flats he had identified, I took one look at the first place and said, "I'll take it." It had a bed, I noticed, and a door which could be locked to keep out knife-brandishing hashish dealers, and that was all I was interested in at that point.

After a couple of days of living in the flat, I started to think that there were some additional features I might have looked for had I thought a bit more deeply. To be fair, it did have a couple of other plus points. I found that if I stood on tiptoe at the right angle I could just see a patch of blue sea and a little bit of the port between two adjacent blocks of flats. And if I stood right in the centre of the flat and grabbed a cat by the tip of its tail (as long as it wasn't a particularly big cat), I could swing it all the way round 360 degrees without it hitting anything.

Which was great, but not much use because I didn't have a cat. Otherwise, I felt that there were a few items missing which could have proved useful: a fridge, for example, a cooker that was a bit more sophisticated than the jumped-up Bunsen burner on offer here, and indeed, as someone working as a PE teacher in a hot African country, it might have occurred to me that I could have used a washing system that was slightly more efficient than the peculiar porcelain thing which stood next to the toilet.

This was a cross between a giant's toilet and a midget's bath, and was totally inadequate for washing the caked sweat from my exhausted body at the end of a long, hot working day. The contortions required to get my armpits in position under the pathetic stream of at-best tepid water I sometimes managed to coax from the tap which fed into this ablutory abomination gave me a permanent backache.

So I spent most of my time in the flat thinking about leaving. But with all the other new things I was having to deal with starting my first teaching job on a different continent, the thought of going out and finding a new flat for myself seemed way too daunting. Inertia was my flatmate.

Until one weekend when Burnsey came up from Rabat.

After a convivial night out on the town, we came back to the flat, had a couple more drinks, sat round talking, and finally went to bed. Surprisingly, in such a cramped place, the bed was, if not exactly a double, wide enough for two people at a pinch. As we lay there in the dark, we continued to talk about nothing in particular, and eventually Burnsey said, "Do you know I've got a bit of a sixth sense?"

Although I hadn't been acquainted with him for too long, I already knew him well enough to know that he was a total bullshitter, and since I was drifting off to sleep, my only response was to think drowsily, "What bollocks is he going to come up with now?"

"I've got a bad feeling about this place."

I still said nothing, and indeed was barely paying any attention.

He was also quiet for a while, and then he said, "I mean it. Something very bad happened... right here in this room."

I was instantly struck by a thunderbolt. In a flash, I knew with total certainty that he was right. Not only that, but I knew what had happened. A woman had been murdered. In that very bed, a woman had been stabbed; she lay on her back, and a man sitting astride her plunged a knife into her heart.

The reason why I knew this so surely was that for the briefest of instants *I was that woman*. I saw that man with the knife raised above me, and my mind experienced the utter horror of it. I did not know the background, but all the anger and confusion that had led up to this event were there, in a jumbled knot in my mind. And I also felt the dreadful knowledge that the crisis of the conflict had arrived, that there was no turning back, and that the very next thing she – and I – would feel would be awful pain followed probably by death.

With a huge mental effort, I forced the horrible image from my consciousness. Nothing even remotely like this had ever happened to me before, but there was not the slightest shadow of doubt in my mind that the woman's murder had really occurred. It was not just something conjured up by a tired and rather inebriated, and perhaps suggestible, imagination. There was something about the way the whole thing took over my mind like a lightning strike, and the vivid and incredibly intense nature of the experience, which left me totally convinced of its reality.

I lay there in the dark. My mind felt almost bruised, and delicate and unstable. I felt that at any second, it could switch back there again, and I fought with all my mental strength to keep it secure. I surrounded it with an iron ring, and concentrated hard to prevent the vision returning. I did not allow myself to think about it at all, and in the stillness of the unlit room, I silently begged Burnsey not to say anything else. Apart from not wanting to ever again experience anything so horrible, I was also terribly aware that the next thing that was going to happen was that the woman was going to die, and it seemed a distinct possibility that if I went back into her brain, I might die too.

Ken didn't speak again, and soon enough I realized that he was asleep. I lay for a long time fighting to keep my mind intact, trying to think of mundane things, until eventually, completely exhausted, I too drifted off.

In the morning, as soon as I woke, I knew immediately that I had to put the iron ring in place around my brain again. I refused to allow myself to think about what I had felt. It was there, like some unspeakable creature lurking in the dark woods at the edge of the meadows. Yet I felt more in control in the daylight, and I knew that as long as I didn't go near the woods, as long as I didn't even think about what had happened, I was safe.

I said nothing to Burnsey about it, and to my relief he seemed to have forgotten about whatever it was, if it was anything, that had made him say what he had said.

That night, I had to sleep again in that bed, in the dark, all on my own. But by then my mind was strong enough, and it was quite easy for me to simply not think about the evil thing in the woods and that kept it at bay.

I followed the same strategy every subsequent night, but of course I never again felt at all comfortable in that flat, and when the opportunity serendipitously arose to move, I did not hesitate. I never asked anyone, or did anything, to try to find out if there had been a murder in that flat, partly because I didn't want to know more, but mostly because the experience had been so real that I didn't need any confirmation.

Shortly afterwards, a guy I knew called Philip approached me during the badminton evening and asked if by any chance I would like to move into their house because they had the opportunity to move to a bigger place but couldn't move out unless they found someone else to take over theirs. I had been round there for tea once, and I seemed to recall that it wasn't a bad place, and so it proved. It had a garden, of sorts, and probably enough room to tie a piece of string a yard long to the tail of a still putative cat and swing it around without harming it. Much.

"It's lovely," said Philip. "The landlord is a right character, and you've got Jim and Jean living next door and they are a wonderful couple. They spend half the year in California and half the year here, and they'll be back in a few weeks."

The formalities were soon sorted out, and I moved in. It was indeed lovely, up to a point. It was a nice old French colonial style house up on the hill next to the Hotel Bristol. But it too had a couple of drawbacks.

The landlord proved to indeed be quite a 'character'. Perhaps an older, wiser fellow than I, one slightly less wet between the ears, would have realized that when someone who wants you to move into their house to help them out describes the landlord not as 'very nice', or 'really helpful', or 'no problem at all', but as 'a right character', alarm bells should go off. Alarm bells really should have gone off about Mohamed Zubair, along with sirens, buzzers and flashing lights.

Rumour was that many years ago, as a poor young lad from the medina, he had exploited his dashing good looks to get a job as a driver for a rich Scottish widow who had come out to live in Tangier. No one will be surprised to learn that the driver very quickly began to deliver other services, and it wasn't long before they were married. Zubair suggested they buy this nice little old French house, but explained that Moroccan law would not let a foreigner own property, so the house had to be in his name. The next step was to persuade her to sign all her assets over to him, to avoid punitive taxes, and then the trap was sprung. The woman was simply thrown out of the house, and Zubair was a wealthy man.

Sometime later on, Zubair decided to build himself a new three storey house in the garden of the old one. So when I moved in, the garden was just a tiny patch of land with a few stunted orange trees, completely overshadowed by a vile concrete block, and the view from the lovely first floor balcony was no longer the sweeping vista of the bay but that same concrete block. Jim and Jean lived on the bottom floor of the new building, and Zubair occupied the top two floors.

The first time I met him was when I signed the papers to rent the old house. I climbed a set of outside steps from the little courtyard which the two houses shared, and rang the bell. I was let in a by a very shy and very attractive young Moroccan maid, who ushered me into a room full of the most garish furniture of the kind which people with no taste who want to show how rich they have become often choose. A slight man in his forties soon appeared and introduced himself warmly as Mohamed. He had a flashing but insincere smile, high cheekbones which gave him somewhat the look of a fox, cold and calculating brown eyes, and long thick black hair oiled and swept back across the top of his head. The maid crept in with a tray of the ubiquitous mint tea, and while we sipped it Zubair exuded bonhomie and welcome. He professed himself delighted to be getting a new tenant from such an august establishment as the American School, and even more so when he found out where I was from because he had a soft spot for the British.

I had not at this point heard any of the stories about him, so my eyebrow remained totally unraised when he had the gall to say "My wife is Scottish actually. You'll have to meet her, although she spends most of her time in Gib these days." I later learned from Rachid that the poor woman lived a hand-to-mouth existence in a poky little flat on Gibraltar, subsisting barely on the pittance which Zubair grudgingly allowed her to have from her own fortune. Zubair voluntarily offered to have the interior of the house repainted as soon as he could get it organized, expansively told me not to worry too much about rent payment deadlines but just to get it to him when it was convenient, issued a sweeping general invitation to come up for tea any time because he loved speaking to the British, and then I escaped. Even before I learned of his background that night at The Nautilus, I felt utterly repelled by the man. He had an indefinable air of the predator, and I was in no doubt that he regarded me as a particularly wholesome piece of potential prey.

Anyway, it was too late to change my mind, and I was installed that afternoon. Since everything I owned had been carried across Europe in a backpack, the moving process was not as complicated as it might have been, and the services of the local equivalent of Pickford's were not required. Incredibly, though, since my paltry salary barely allowed me to buy enough food to keep me alive, I had somehow managed to acquire a few more things than would fit in the backpack; but even so it was nothing that a few plastic bags and a taxi could not handle in one trip.

With a chance to have a good look around the place, I found that the upstairs, consisting of two bedrooms, a lounge area, and a balcony (with the, sadly, now extremely restricted view), was perfectly pleasant. I installed my portable stereo (which had occupied about seventy per cent of the space in my backpack all the way from England), slapped in a tape, and with 'It's Only Rock 'n' Roll' belting out I went back to check out the downstairs. This was a disappointment.

The washing arrangements, a 'shower' consisting of a hole in the wall out of which poured water which could be either cold or scalding, were, whilst admittedly an improvement, still not utopian. The kitchen was a large room with a grimy gas cooker and quite a few dilapidated cupboards. The big problem here was that the room was utterly windowless (the wall where the original window had been had evidently been replaced by the new wall of Chateau Zubair) and the one feeble light in the corner was totally inadequate.

Perhaps it was the heady excitement of having a real house all to myself that persuaded me that a spot of simple DIY here could affect an improvement. Although I had had more of what you might call a classical than a practical education, and despite a distinct lack of experience in the handyman domain, I was confident that with the application of a combination of intelligence and good old common sense, I could solve the problem of the poor lighting in the kitchen.

I had a big advantage because the wiring system was perfectly easy to fathom since, in true Third World style, it was all draped around on the outside of the walls. There was a massive junction box over in one corner, with wires protruding in all directions and heading off all over the house. One of these wires went across the ceiling and passed through a crude hole above the back door out into the yard where it obviously fed a light out in the courtyard.

After a careful analysis, therefore, I formulated a plan: branch into the wire which crossed the ceiling and run a light bulb from it. I reckoned that all I had to do was turn off the power (obviously), then cut in to the wire, attach it to a light fitting I could cannibalise from somewhere else in the house, and attach a bulb. Simple.

The box in the corner had all kinds of strange buttons and levers on it, but it also contained a massive red switch smack in the middle. This was obviously an on-off switch. (I hope I'm not getting too technical for my readers here.) I pushed it up, and it clunked solidly off. I then went around the house and tried several lights, and they were all dead, so I felt confident in approaching my target wire. I stood on a chair, reached up and grabbed the wire with my left hand, and sawed into it with my Swiss knife. A massive jolt shot up my right arm, palpably slammed into my shoulder joint, and bounced back down my arm again.

As I picked myself up from the opposite corner of the room, I felt a mixture of well, shock obviously, and aggrievement. After early establishment of the fact that I didn't seem to have suffered any permanent damage (it was my immediate belief that my shoulder joint, which I had felt repel the electrical pulse, had prevented it getting to my heart and probably stopping it), I stared up at the offending wire.

I had switched off all the power, and had even tested to make sure that there was no electricity coming out of that junction box. I examined the switch again, and it was still clearly up in the off position. I tried a few lights again and none of them worked. It was a complete mystery. I was beginning to think that the only possible explanation was that, although I had turned off the electricity, there had still been a little bit left in the wire when I had cut into it, when the real solution dawned on me. That wire was not carrying electricity OUT of the box to the courtyard light; it was carrying electricity IN to the box from the mains supply outside.

I decided not to try any more DIY, and managed to produce all my culinary concoctions thereafter in a satisfactory manner, despite the gloom.

Jim and Jean, my mythical neighbours, owned a nice little open topped American sports car, which sat in the courtyard under a dustsheet during their sojourn over in California. One day I came walking up the street on my way home from work to see the car out in the road and a man sitting at the wheel, so I strode up confidently and said "Hello. My name is Rob, and I'm your neighbour. You must be Jim."

"No. I'm Gene."

I should have guessed really, Tangier being the place it was.

Jim and Gene were a lovely couple, though, showing that Philip hadn't been completely awry in his comments on my future neighbours. They were in their sixties, and like pretty well all of the expatriate denizens of the city in those days, they were perhaps a little too fond of a drink, but I used to pop in for a beer occasionally when I got home from work, and I enjoyed their company. Jim, I think it was, but it might have been Gene, did once ask me with a bit of a glint in his eye which way my proclivities lay, but, on learning that it was not his way, merely said, "A shame" with a sigh, and the subject was never again broached.

One Saturday night, Jim and Gene went out to a party. It was quite a posh do, and Jim, or it might have been Gene, put on his best suit. At the party, he ate a lot of food, and drank an even 'lotter' of a number of different alcoholic concoctions, the result being that he began to feel unwell and decided to go home. He staggered back on his own (luckily, the party was somewhere nearby), but before he could make it to a refuge, it all caught up with him, and he threw up all down his front. He barely had enough energy to stumble to the bathroom, but he made it, where he had the presence of mind to run a bath and leave his messed up suit to soak, to be dealt with later, while he quickly showered and went to bed.

In the morning, the old Moroccan woman they employed to clean their house arrived and let herself quietly in. She was quite used to going about her business while the masters slept in, sometimes well into the afternoon, and so she set off to quietly tidy the place up. But when she came to the bathroom, she took one look at the suit floating in the water and thought it was a body. Convinced that one of the monsieurs had drowned in the bath, she ran out into the courtyard emitting a bloodcurdling wail.

Moroccan women possess an incredible ability – natural or learned I know not – to wail. They usually confine themselves to big family events like weddings and funerals, but hysteria can set in at any time. If you think of something between a shriek and a moan you won't really be anywhere near understanding the sound, but those are the closest words I can come up with. I think 'ululate' might also apply, but I'm not sure.

Suffice to say that my own mid-Sunday morning slumber was rudely awakened in the most alarming manner. I rushed down to the courtyard, arriving at about the same time as Zubair and a bleary Jim, or etc. The woman, dressed in a grey djellaba and with her head covered by a white scarf, was keening wildly and shrilly, her hands alternating between holding her head and

162

beating her breast. Zubair shouted at her in Arabic, but to no avail. Jim (perhaps) shouted at her in Californian, to equal avail. Not to be outdone, and just in case there might be someone somewhere in North Africa or the Iberian Peninsula who had not yet heard the commotion, I joined in and shouted at her in Yorkshire. But the availness remained stubbornly on zero.

Gene, or – oh I wish I'd never started this, let's just say the other one – finally stumbled out of their door, at the sight of whom the woman's wailing became even more hysterical and shrill. While the latest arrival dutifully joined in the avail-less shouting competition, the poor distraught creature, pointing in horror at Gene (we'll say) backed towards the gate, where her path was fortunately blocked by a growing crowd of passers-by. Finally, Zubair managed to adroitly manoeuvre his way between the flailing arms and grab her in a bear hug, and very slowly his whispered calming words in her ear soothed her hysteria. Her incoherent wails subsided until we could make out the sobbing repetition of the word *humba*, ghost.

Well of course in the end we got her calmed down and the whole misunderstanding was straightened out, poor Fatima was sent home to recover, and we all had a good chuckle about it.

Except that the next day, Zubair appeared on Jim and Gene's doorstep with a very grave look on his face. He informed them in the most tragic tone that the whole incident had caused his wife so much stress that she had had a miscarriage. When Jim/Gene overcame their incredulity enough to point out that his wife was in Gibraltar, Zubair replied that no, he was referring to Leila. Leila was the 15-year-old girl who we all assumed was Zubair's maid, but he was now claiming was not only his wife but had until the day before been pregnant with what Zubair fervently hoped would be his long-awaited first born son.

He was now demanding two thousand dollars in compensation. They, of course, did not believe a word of it, and flatly refused to pay, but several weeks later, I learned that they had given Zubair a couple of hundred just to keep him quiet.

Trois petit pieces de bois

One day, a fellow wearing a white linen suit appeared on the edge of the court while I was teaching some seventh and eighth graders the rudiments of volleyball. It turned out that he was from the British Consulate. HMS *Forester* was apparently due to dock in the port in a couple of weeks' time, and AST were hereby challenged to a football match v Forester FC. I looked at my diary and saw that we didn't have a game on the day in question, so I agreed to the contest.

A few days later, I was very pleased to receive an official invitation to a reception at the British Consulate, hosted by Captain Caruthers or some such, on the evening following the game.

The day in question was a Wednesday, and after school was finished, my lads went into the locker room and then emerged in dribs and drabs, wearing the red shirt and white shorts which, sad to say, was our school kit. (My campaign to change the colours to white, with a blue and gold trim, had foundered on the twin rocks of tradition and lack of finance.)

I had learned from experience that any attempt to persuade them to stretch or do any organised preparation for the game was doomed to failure, so I watched, grinding my teeth a little, as they all congregated on the edge of the box and fired shots at the empty net (even the keeper wanted to shoot), ninety-nine of which sailed miles over the bar, the ball ending up in the orange grove behind the pitch where it stayed while they argued over who should retrieve it. The, to me, obvious solution, that the player who kicked it should go and get it, did not seem to occur to them. They preferred a system whereby the youngest player fetched it, unless he was really fed up at having just fetched the previous ten balls, in which case, occasionally, the next youngest would be prevailed upon to do the job.

Eventually, our yellow school bus, which I had dispatched to the port, rolled back into the car park, and the pride of the British navy alighted and went to get changed.

The game, even though it was literally a case of men against boys, proceeded well. Each team possessed very distinct qualities. Speed and skill on the one hand, experience, aggression and strength on the other, and they balanced themselves out pretty evenly. A few of the sailor boys were a bit over the top with their aggression early on (evidently having spent a bit too long cooped up on the high seas), but they responded very well to a quiet word from me reminding them that they were only playing boys. Some of the language was also a trifle salty, but if any of the navy lads understood Arabic, they didn't seem to take offence.

As ever, I found the task of reffing a game whilst at the same time coaching one of the teams to be difficult, but I just tried to honestly call everything I saw as fairly as I could. I think if anything, in this and in all the other games when I had to do both tasks, I actually favoured the opposition, due to a subconscious desire not to seem biased towards my team. This game seemed to be heading towards a 1-1 draw when, in the very last minute, a dreadfully mistimed tackle felled El Habsi as he dribbled into the box. I had to give a penalty, and the decision was accepted most sportingly by the Foresters. To my surprise, though, the normally infallible and unflappable Lamarti demonstrated that all that pre-match practice had not been the waste of time I had thought it to be by depositing the ball deep into the orange grove.

A very diplomatic and fair result, then. The Foresters presented us with a nice ship's plaque, and before they left they invited me on board the next evening to drink some English beer, an invitation which I gratefully accepted.

After everyone had gone, and with several hours to kill before the reception, I decided to go over to the dorm and call on my friend and colleague, Boston Bill Gurney.

Bill and I had a lot in common. We had arrived in Tangier at the same time, we were both starting our first ever teaching job and we shared a somewhat sceptical view of pedagogy as a profession.

Bill taught first grade. Whenever he couldn't take being confined in a room with eleven six-year-olds any longer, he would take them all outside, borrow a ball from me, kick it as far as he could into the orange grove, and tell them all to race after it and see who could bring it back to him. Whereupon he would kick it back into the grove again, repeating the process ad infinitum, or ad the little buggers were exhausted. Then he'd take them back inside for nap time.

Bill was the first member of the American species I had ever properly known, and I was his first real Englishman, so we both found each other quite fascinating. (Of course, I later learned that by no means all Americans are anywhere near as weird as he was, and he must have been disappointed to find that not all English people are as cool, sophisticated and intelligent as I am.)

Anyway, at this particular time, Vince Hilaire, the vice principal who was also the head of the dorm, was off on some trip to the Far East, and Bill was filling in for him. The downside of this was that he had to supervise the handful of miserable and disaffected teenagers whose parents had abandoned them into the 'care' of AST. The upside was that he got to use Hilaire's splendid suite of rooms in the dorm.

Which was why I decided to drop in on him after the Foresters game.

He greeted me with the information that he had just "rustled up a batch of margaritas." It turned out that Hilaire, perhaps unwisely, had told Bill to make himself completely at home in his apartment, and to use anything he found in there; and Bill had just discovered a large supply of gin. When concocting his margaritas, he had erred dramatically, ingredients-wise, on the side of the gin, given that he had rare access to free bottles of the stuff, and it was expensive gin, too. The result was that his so-called 'margarita' was in fact virtually neat gin, and it packed a kick like a Peter Lorimer special.

Fresh from my endeavours on a very hot afternoon on the pitch, I was extremely thirsty, so the first drink Bill poured for me disappeared down my throat without touching the sides, thereby bypassing the taste buds which would surely have warned me that I was consuming something lethal. It wasn't until about half way through the fourth drink that I slowed up enough to notice that I was drinking rocket fuel, and I barely had time to utter a murmur of protest before I passed out.

I woke up ninety minutes later. Dazed and confused, I think, is the phrase to describe my condition, but once I had figured out where I was, who I was with, and why my head was gyrating, I looked at my watch and cried out, "Shit! I'm supposed to be at the British Consulate in twenty-five minutes!"

To get myself back to my flat, shower, change, and then get to the Consulate in that time would have been beyond even Billy Whizz, let alone Rob Heath after having guzzled virtually half a bottle of gin. But Gurney, who had a lot of redeeming to do since I felt he was entirely responsible for my plight with his reckless drink concocting antics, clawed back a few of the very many points he had lost with a brilliant suggestion.

"Hey! Hilaire told me to use anything of his that I liked. Well, you're about his size, so why don't you go in some of his clothes?"

Not only was he about my size, he also possessed a vastly superior wardrobe than did I. I had a rapid shower and then selected a very smart outfit of trousers, shirt and tie. Even his shoes fitted reasonably comfortably, and the final touch was a jacket. Hilaire's jackets were neatly hanging in a row in his wardrobe, and it was clear that the creamy tweed one was the perfect selection to round off my ensemble.

Luck was with me, because the school is in a bit of a backwater where taxis didn't frequently tread, but I walked out of the gate and, for the one and only time when I really needed a cab, one came by straight away. Miraculously, I got to the consulate just a few, rather fashionable I thought, minutes late. Within half an hour of waking in a strange and alarmingly whirling apartment and a state of panic, here I was looking as sharp as a pointed stick, circulating amongst the great and the good while waiters pressed further helpings of gin on me. I felt brilliant.

Until a voice suddenly boomed across the room, "Who's that wearing Vince Hilaire's jacket?"

Instantly, the murmur of chitchat was silenced. A large man standing on the far side of the room was pointing an accusing finger, and everyone turned to stare at me. As luck would have it, I had just grabbed two gin fizzes from a waiter (because, excellent though the serving staff were, I feared that in the general melee it might take a while before one passed near me again.) So I stood there, a glass in each hand, with everyone glaring with hostility at me. Apparently, some form of explanation was required, but all I could think of was how the fuck did that old fart know I was wearing Hilaire's stupid bastard jacket?

"Young man, explain yourself. Who are you, and why are you wearing Vince Hilaire's jacket?"

As I mumbled something pathetic about him having lent it to me, it occurred to me that my invitation to the reception, which would have established my identity and right to be there, was back at my flat.

"What's that you say, boy? He lent it to you? Are you sure about that? It seems very unlikely to me."

Just as I was thinking that a desperate escape ('Wait a minute, is this the *British* Consulate? How silly of me, I'm at the wrong party! I'm supposed to be at the Lithuanian! I'll be off then.') might be my only hope of avoiding arrest for the, apparently, suddenly heinous crime of jacket theft, and wondering whether I could get away with knocking back my two gins en route for the door, the navy officer standing next to the fat accusing git suddenly said, "Why you're the sports teacher up at the American School aren't you?"

Instantly, the whole drama ended. The show was over. One word of recognition from a monkey in a fancy uniform and I was no longer an obvious freeloading, gate-crashing, thieving impostor. Everyone returned to their suspended conversations about how degenerate, disorganised or dishonest are all Moroccans, and I was able to make my way across the room to where my nemesis and my saviour stood. On the way, my, by this point seriously befuddled brain, managed to figure out one thing: that the man who had saved me was the ship's liaison officer, who had been at the school in the afternoon watching the game.

It turned out that the florid-faced bastard with the very loud voice and equally suspicious nature was Lord Riever, a famous resident of Tangier and former Tory minister. I had heard of him, but it seemed our social circles were not congruent. Hilaire, on the other hand, was apparently big buddies with him; such big buddies, in fact, that he had visited the Riever stately home in

Scotland, where he had been presented with a jacket made from the Riever family's official (and unique) tweed. Riever, who still bore a very hostile air, explained all this to me, and took great pains to point out that it was a very expensive jacket and he was extremely surprised that Hilaire had agreed to lend it to me.

Luckily, before I was called on to make any further explanations, a gong sounded, and we were all requested to file through to the massive long dining table and to find our assigned seat. I hastily complied, and found myself happily placed well down the table away from the likes of Riever and the other big nobs.

Kevin Sharp was sitting on my right.

Kevin was a young English lad, about the same age as me, whose uncle owned a superb villa up on the mountain. They were obviously extremely well off, and Kevin came out to Tangier for quite long spells, apparently whenever the urge came upon him to do so. I had seen him around town a few times, and had conversed with him on occasion, but you couldn't say that we were friends. If you could say that we were friends, then you would expect that if one of those friends was a poverty-stricken educator living in a hovel, whilst the other had a magnificent villa, then the latter would invite the former up to his palace to enjoy the pool, and to sip Pimm's on the terrace overlooking the Straits. But that never happened, so you can rest easy if you ever do say that we were not friends, safe in the knowledge that you won't be telling a lie.

When we did speak, as indeed we were constrained to do now, finding ourselves juxtaposed, we usually talked about British sport, and on this occasion, I was very keen to hear about how the summer's test cricket was progressing, since Kevin had not only been back during the early part of the series, he had actually been to Lord's ("my uncle is a member of MCC") for a couple of days of the First Test, whilst I had been subsisting on a starvation diet of week-old reports from highly intermittent Daily Telegraphs.

Sitting opposite Kevin was Lamine Sakho, who was something at the French Consulate. He had been involved in a three-way discussion about quelquechose with some people further down the table, but when that petered out, or I suppose, since it had been carried out in French, I should say pierred out, he turned and cocked an oreille to our conversation. Divining soon enough that we were talking about cricket, he jumped in with, "Ah, le cricket. C'est quel espece de jeu?"

I responded, in my best French, with a shrug. But Kevin, whose foolhardiness obviously outstripped even his stinginess in inviting people round to his sumptuous villa, embarked, without a deuxieme pense, on what must surely have been one of the most impossible tasks ever carried out in the history of international relations; he tried to explain the laws and traditions of cricket, in French (which he didn't speak very well anyway) to a Frenchman. All I could do was sit back, shake my head, and observe.

"Okay. Er, right, em... il y a trois petit pieces de bois. Et a l'autre fin il y a aussi er la meme. Et il y a deux plus petit pieces de bois qui sont placé au dessus de les autres pieces. Et ca s'appelle le wicket, ou, erm... la porte, oui c'est ca."

Lamine's eyes were already glazing over, but being a diplomat I suppose it was his metier (or whatever the French is for that) to maintain a show of interest, even if it was only a facade (or whatever etc.), whilst his interlocutor rambled on interminably.

Opposite me, I had been surprised to see, was the consul general's wife, Antonia Currie. Whether she had been placed down amongst the lower ranks to keep order, or because her husband was punishing her for some marital or diplomatic gaffe, I could not divine, but I did notice that she had just tuned out of a discussion on her right, and was turning her best, 'And what do you do?' face to me.

"And what do you do?" she asked, predictably.

I was then granted the regulation two and a half minutes to burble about my job while she projected her 'how marvellous' face at me, interspersed with encouraging nods and smiles, and then with a "Lovely," she turned to a gentleman along from me with a gambit about the severity of the recent rains.

To my right, l'histoire de cricket was still under way.

A salt cellar, a pepper pot and a vinegar bottle had been pressed into service. "Mais," Kevin was saying. "On ne peut pas etre hors jambe avant porte si la balle touche la terre dehors la ligne de la stump de jambe." He indicated with his finger a spot on the tablecloth where, if the sundry items he had placed there had been stumps, and if a ball had landed at that spot and bounced towards those stumps, and if a tiny imaginary batsman had been there, and the ball had hit his pads, the imaginary batsman would not have been out. Then he looked up into the face of Lamine, wearing an expression of sincere earnestness, his eyebrows raised, and a slightly questioning smile on his lips. His expression said, 'Now I've made this so simple even a cockroach could

174

probably understand it, so you see exactly what I mean, right?' He was met, surprisingly enough, by a look of total Gallic bemusement.

"Voyez!" he said, and, grabbing a napkin holder, he placed two fingers of his left hand in front of the strategically placed condiments. "Ca," he said, waggling his fingers, "est le batsman, err, l'homme de bat. Et ca," holding up the napkin holder, "est la balle. Si la balle touche la terre ici," and he swept the napkin holder through the air with his right hand, "et si il frappe le monsieur sur la jambe apres," and he moved the 'ball' on to knock against his finger, "il n'est PAS jambe avant porte."

"Even if, er..." He turned to me. "How do you say 'even if' in French?"

"Errr, I don't know, erm..."

"Meme si," said Sakho.

"Oh, right, thanks. Meme," he added triumphantly, taking away his fingers and running the 'ball' through its course again, "si la balle va frapper la porte!" And he knocked the napkin holder against the leg stump.

Except of course it wasn't a leg stump. It was a little bottle of vinegar which someone had negligently failed to put the little cork stopper properly back into. And so when it fell over, after having been frapped by a balle, the stopper jumped out and vinegar spurted out all over the cream cotton dress of Mrs Her Britannic Majesty's Consul General.

"Comment est-il?" I murmured to myself.

Two weeks of debauchery

When I was at university in Leeds, I ended up living in a terraced house in the Woodhouse area of the city. It was Number 6, Burchett Grove, and during the three years I lived there, that house became the headquarters for a tremendous series of japes. A strange cast of characters came and went during that time, but the core members, who came to be known, along with me, as the Burchett Boys, were Mike Neary, Rich Pinder, and Alan Grant.

I kept up a correspondence with these three reprobates after I left for Morocco, although their rather cavalier approach to the conventions of the postal system proved to be a bit of a stumbling block to the smoothness of our communication.

Pinder claimed to have sent me a card addressed to:

ROB HEATH,
1, MUD HUT LANE,
TANGIER,
MOROCCO.

Neary replied to a letter I had written him on headed school notepaper, and he had the bright idea of laboriously and meticulously copying down the peculiar squiggles of the school address as it appeared on the notepaper in Arabic, and sending it off. Unfortunately, the Arabic address on AST paper was written all across one line at the top, and Mike failed to take into account the fact that Arabic is written from right to left. Of course, even if he had transcribed the script correctly, there was still the problem of what the Post Office workers in Chelsea were supposed to make of an envelope addressed like that. Incredibly, though, and I think this is a remarkable testament to the dedication and perseverance of myriad members of the postal profession, I did eventually receive the letter. It took ten months to get to me, and by reading the profusion of franking stamps on the envelope, I deduced that it had been sent to Mauretania, at least, before ending up with me.

But we did manage to maintain a semblance of normal communication, and one topic we discussed in our letters was the idea of a Burchett Tour to Tangier. I had received a few intimations that such a trip was being planned at their end, and then one day, I got a postcard from Pinder bearing only the message 'WATCH OUT, WE'RE ON OUR WAY'.

The poor saps thought it would be a jolly wheeze to simply turn up in Tangier, and surprise me. They planned to stroll out of the airport and give my address to a taxi driver, who would deliver them to my door. They had no concept of the reality of Morocco; of the fact that first of all the chances of the taxi driver even being able to read or understand the address they were giving him were nil, and second, the chances, even if he did comprehend, of him being able to find an address like that were even less than nil.

So when they walked out of the terminal building, approached the first taxi driver they saw, and showed him my address, it has to register as a miracle that he said to them in English "Okay, I can get you there, no problem," and he did.

Unfortunately, that is where their luck ran out.

They arrived on my doorstep at about seven p.m. on a Friday evening, half an hour after I had set off with Boston Bill for a session of Tom Collinses at Madame Porte's teahouse. Slightly deflated to find no one home, they nevertheless made themselves comfortable on the pavement and waited patiently for my return, all the time anticipating with excitement how surprised I would be to find them there.

But after a pretty heavy intake of cocktails, followed by a very congenial meal (with extras) at Rachid's, and then repairing to Gurney's flat (which was conveniently located two doors from The Nautilus) I put my feet up on his couch, just for a couple of minutes, and didn't wake up until the morning.

The three adventurers stuck it out until after midnight and then, concluding that I had gone away for the weekend, took a cab into town and checked in to a cheap hotel.

The following morning, I bade farewell to the comatose Gurney, and sauntered up onto Rue Pasteur. I stopped at a kiosk and discovered a rare gem: an only four-days-old copy of *The Guardian*! Snapping it up, I immediately repaired to a table outside the Café des Sports, ordered a coffee and croissant, and immersed myself in the paper.

I usually had to make do with the *Daily Telegraph*, a paper which I utterly despised and would not have used to wipe my arse with back in England, but it was the only sample of the English press which usually made its way out to Tangier, and if I wanted to keep up with the important news (i.e. how Leeds United and/or Yorkshire CCC were getting on) I was a beggar who could not afford to be a chooser. Reading the *Telegraph*, and the horrible small-minded narrow attitudes it espoused, did have the merit of reminding me, if I needed to be reminded (which I didn't) exactly why I was glad not to be living in England anymore.

But *The Guardian*! Not only was it only found on the Tangerine newsstands very seldom, it also provided a luxurious dip into all that was good about English culture, with its wit, its erudition, and its free-thinking approach. As I sat reading the paper, I metaphorically drew it round me like a deep velvet cloak, and totally immersed myself in a cocoon of the best of *home*.

Of course, on top of its deliberate wit, *The Guardian* in those days, before the onset of computer typesetting, word processing, and suchlike spoilsport inventions, was notorious for the inadvertent hilarity of its misprints, and on that occasion I discovered a classic. The cricket correspondent, phoning in his report on the Test Match from Edgbaston, had evidently intended to praise Geoff Boycott for the *aplomb* with which he conducted his innings, but the typist on the other end of the line had apparently got the wrong end of the stick. I therefore read, to my surprise, that, 'Boycott, batting with a plum, compiled a fluent unbeaten half century before the close.'

As I was enjoying my three Cs – coffee, croissant, and home culture – Mike Neary, leaving the other two sleeping, emerged from their hotel and decided to take a stroll around the town and see how the land lay. What were the chances, in a city of two million inhabitants, that he should bump into the one person they had come to see? But he did! He spotted me sitting at my table and, after a quick double take, managed to execute the coolest greeting since Stanley in the jungle. Rather than rush over to me yelling my name in amazement and relief that he had located me and they now had somewhere to stay, he simply sidled up and said, "Excuse me, don't I know you?"

I looked up from my musings, in which I had been trying to conjure up an image of Geoff Boycott walking out to bat against the fearsome West Indies' attack with a small piece of soft fruit instead of a bat, in astonishment and delight to find Mike standing there.

We had soon reunited with the other two, decamped from the hotel, and were all happily installed chez moi; then we started making plans for two weeks of serious debauchery.

We agreed that hashish should be the first order of business, so we decided to lunch at Rachid's, and Farid supplied us with a splendid slab of sweet-smelling, turd-coloured Moroccan hashish of the highest quality. Back at the flat, we worried rather about what to do with it. It was going to last us all fortnight, but the other lads were convinced, having heard too many horror stories about drugbusts and Moroccan jails, that the police might raid us and find it. We thought up all manner of hiding places for it, but each one seemed to be exactly the place where raiding police would look first. Eventually, we hit upon the perfect solution, based on the concept that the police would look in all the obvious hiding places, but would probably not notice anything right in front of their noses. (I must admit, we had been smoking the stuff quite a bit by this time.) So we stuck it in the middle of a bare expanse of wall with a piece of blutack, and just to make doubly sure that it was so obvious no policeman would notice it, we stuck a piece of paper next to it with an arrow and the word 'DRUGS'.

One minor problem of the Burchett Boys' unannounced visit was that I was still at work. Had they discussed the matter with me, I would have told them to come during the summer vacation, but oh no, they thought they knew best. So, although I did have a great time while they were there, it was the toughest two weeks to get through.

The flat I lived in by that point (#3 abode) contained one double bed, one sofa and, er... that was about it. So the sleeping arrangements for a team of four big lurgs were a bit problematical.

Since I had to get up for work, the three visitors generously allowed me to sleep in my own bed. The other three rotated each night; one would join me in the double bed, one would sleep on the sofa, and one on the floor. In the morning, when I got up, after a minimal amount of sleep, and left for work, the one on the floor would move into my place on the bed. Someone was usually happily installed and sleeping luxuriantly in my spot before I had even finished shaving and dressing, prior to dragging my weary body off to inculcate lissom youths with healthy fitness habits. I would walk in the door at the end of the day like a zombie, totally drained, to find the lads had just showered, after sleeping all day, and were ready to head out to start having fun all over again. Any pleas on my part for permission to have a power nap, or a chance to regenerate a little, were rudely rejected.

One night, we flagged down a cab outside the flat and set off into town. Grant was in the middle of telling us a story about how he had been thrown out of a girlfriend's house after her father caught him pissing in a potted plant, and I was so caught up in the narrative that I omitted to take the first rudimentary precaution against being fleeced like a tourist, i.e. I forgot to insist that the driver turn on his meter. When we arrived and climbed out, I glanced at the meter and only then realised my folly.

The fare should have been about one dirham sixty, and I usually gave two dirhams if the driver had not been too manic, but without any figure on the meter, this guy asked me for ten dirhams. I of course told him in no uncertain terms that we were not tourists, that I knew what the fare should have been, and that there was no way he was getting ten dirhams. At this, he leaped out of his cab and started yelling at me with terrible ferocity. It was the old wild-eyed rage act, designed to make tourists think that they really were cheating the guy if they didn't pay what he asked, and it impressed me not one jot. I fished in my pocket for a couple of coins, tossed them onto the passenger seat through the window, pulled my arm from his grasp, and set off to join the others, who had headed up a side street.

Just after I caught up with them, I heard heavy steps behind me, and I turned round to see the taxi driver brandishing a very nasty-looking curved bladed knife.

He stood, breathing heavily, holding the knife out in front of him, with a, frankly, murderous gleam in his eye. But I couldn't believe the melodrama of it all. I was well aware that eight dirhams meant a lot more to him than it did to me, but was he really going to murder me in broad daylight in the street over such a sum? I don't know if it was me laughing at him, or the realization that my mates were all big lads, but after volleying a couple of choice curses at me in Arabic, and spitting on the ground, he turned and went muttering back to his cab, letting rip with the odd embellishment to the curses over his shoulder on the way.

We were headed to a cabaret which I had heard provided a fine spectacle. And indeed it did. The performers were all from Paris, and they put on a superb, and magnificently camp, show, including singing, dancing and various skits, all performed in drag. We were sat near the front, and I had the misfortune to have the aisle seat. I compounded that misfortune by clearly showing that I was enjoying the show tremendously. I didn't know then, but I do now, that this made me a sitting duck.

Near the end of the show, they asked for a volunteer to come on stage to help them. Before I knew what was happening, one of the performers materialized next to me and pulled me out of my seat, and the next thing I knew I was up on the stage. They proceeded to pretend to teach me a song, but every time I repeated the line they gave me, they all hooted and insisted that I had got it wrong, and a particularly butch 'mistress' appeared in leather with a whip to chastise me for my mistakes. Finally, they abandoned that song and started another, forcing me to join the dance. But it soon deteriorated into a farce as they managed somehow to tumble me to my knees and immediately the cheekiest chap, dressed in a thin cotton dress and sporting ridiculous false breasts and black stockings, leaped on my back and started humping away.

Grant, Pinder and Neary were unanimous later in their opinion that this performance had been the highlight of their visit, although personally I did not put it even in my top five thousand things that happened during their stay.

A disco on the roof of the biggest package tour hotel in Tangier, The Sultan, was another venue we frequented. We didn't usually stay there long, but one night we ended up there and a couple of English girls took a bit of a shine to Pinder and Grant. When we finally left, I was surprised to find one of these girls was in the taxi with us. She was a large girl whom, you could tell, from the way she was pouring herself all over him, had become firm friends with Rich very quickly. Readers of *Viz* won't believe this, but I swear I recall that her name was Tracy.

Back at the flat, Richard and Tracy ensconced themselves rapidly in the bedroom, and the rest of us made do with what was left.

I woke mercifully late in the morning, it being a Saturday, and started mooching around making coffee and thinking about toast. I tried kicking Grant and Neary, but neither of them seemed inclined to get up, so, forgetting that we had an extra visitor that night, I went into the bedroom to see if Pinder was up. And he was, in a manner of speaking. I was momentarily horrified to find him lying on his back, with the massive body of Tracy enthusiastically athwart him. Just for a second, before I hastily withdrew, he caught my eye, and the look I saw there was one of fear, and almost a plea to be rescued.

Tracy left soon after that, and I think we were all relieved to hear that she was going home that afternoon.

That was the day of the big tennis match.

Strangely, although we were all sports fanatics and had lived in the same house for three years, none of us had ever seen any of the others play tennis. But the subject came up at one point, and as we talked, we realized that each of us was convinced that he was not only an excellent player, but was clearly far superior to the other three. After several rounds of bragging, the idea was hit upon for us to have a match, a best-of-five-sets showdown, and I booked a court at the Italian Club.

It was decided early on that I should partner Neary against the Essex-Scotland combination of Pinder and Grant. This seemed appropriate, because Neary claimed to be 'classically trained' as a tennis player, which seemed to mesh well with my preference for an aggressive serve-and-volley approach. As Mike and I discussed tactics, I could tell that he was indeed clearly a player with a similar outlook to me, and I actually began to feel a bit sorry for the Grinders (as we called them), and hoped our win wouldn't be too embarrassingly easy.

I can't believe now that I didn't see any flashing mental warning lights when Neary told me he was 'classically trained', because I had already been through this with him before, in the context of cricket.

For cricket, too, was a game we had never seen each other play, and in our final month together at Leeds, we had decided to enter our six-a-side football team, BADCO, in the university six-a-side cricket tournament.

Mike had assured me then that, you guessed it, he had received a 'classical' training in the art of batsmanship.

It shouldn't have mattered either way, because I had a school friend who played for Derbyshire Second XI, and he agreed to play in our team as a ringer. With Jeremy on board, we were confident we could beat anyone.

In the first round, we won the toss and batted. I opened with Jeremy, and we scored 72 off our five overs (of which my contribution was a small but, I felt, crucial 9), and the opposition dribbled along to a miserable 30-odd.

In the second round, we lost the toss and had to bowl first. Jeremy was a first class bat, but nothing more than an average bowler, so the bowling bit was something we were slightly worried about; but a splendid team performance in the field restricted the opposition to a paltry 28.

I was leaning casually on my bat at the non-striker's end, wondering if Jeremy would knock off the runs in the very first over, when I saw him hit the third ball straight down a fielder's throat. Jeremy was out! But there was no need to panic, because Mike Neary, the classically trained batsman I had been hearing so much about, was striding to the wicket, and we only needed 21 more runs (Jeremy had hit the first two balls for four) off 32 balls.

However, it appeared that Mike's classical training seemed to have consisted of preparing him to take a step forward, lift his bat with a flourish, swing it in a flowing arc, miss the ball, and look up the wicket with a mystified expression. I could see that there was no use relying on that wanker Neary; if we were going to do this, it was going to be up to me to get it done.

However, the bowling was surprisingly good, and I, despite the vast talent which I had been telling Mike for days that I possessed, couldn't quite manage to connect bat to ball. We were running out of balls, and the target was getting more and more daunting, when I finally hit one. Admittedly, the ball went straight to a fielder, but it was no time to worry about niceties. I called Mike for a single and set off charging down the wicket.

I learned then that Mike's classical training had not extended to the etiquette of running between the wickets. It is universally accepted that when the striker hits the ball in front of the wicket, it is his prerogative to decide whether to run, and it is the job of the non-striker to basically do what he's told. Now admittedly, my shot was not exactly in front of the wicket, but it was definitely squarish. At any rate, given the situation, it was obvious that a good response to your partner shouting YES and running towards you would quite clearly not be to shout back NO, stand still with a look of amazement on your face, then set off with a resigned shrug and only get about five steps down the wicket before they broke the stumps at the other end.

That run-out was the subject of quite a lot of intensive discussion afterwards. Topics such as whose fault it was, and how much it contributed to our defeat, got an exhaustive airing. Indeed, they were still being debated years later, on a different continent, right up to the start of a needle tennis match.

On court at the Italian Club, my confidence grew even more during the knock-up. Admittedly, I looked like the worst player on the court, but I knew once I warmed up that would soon change. Neary seemed to have an idea of the basics, even if he did do everything with a rather pretentious exaggerated flourish and have a laughable service action. Pinder obviously suffered from delusions of grandeur, thinking he was a much better player than he was and attempting outrageous topspin forehands all the time which invariably flew comfortably out. Grant walked on court wearing a pair of filthy once-white rugby shorts, a long-sleeved button-up shirt, a cravat and a bush hat (being Scottish, he was tragically fair of skin, and he had a relationship with the sun rather similar to that of Superman with krypton), and he played exactly like he looked. That is, like a total plonker.

We won the toss, and elected to serve first. I thought it best to let Neary settle his nerves, so I told him I would take on the pressure of serving. Unfortunately, a surprising spate of double-faults saw us lose that game. Mike gave me a bit of a tetchy look, but said, "No problem, Rob, there's a long way to go yet."

Pinder served next, and we were surprised to find his serve was both powerful and accurate. 0-2, but not yet a crisis.

2-5 and 30-40 was a crisis. Grant served, and I hit a skimming forehand return across court. True to my beliefs, I followed it in and joined Mike at the net. Grant, struggling deep behind the baseline, somehow managed to reach the ball and throw up a pretty weak attempt at a lob, which had neither the height nor the depth to cause us any damage. As I backed off to get under the ball and put away the smash, I heard a call of 'MINE'. I hesitated for an instant, but then, realizing that Neary's call was absurd because the ball was so obviously in my zone, I continued my preparation for the smash. Just as I started to throw my racket at the ball, I felt a blow in my back, and Neary's racket came slicing through the air, narrowly missing my head, and pathetically dropped the ball into the net. I ended up on the ground, with Neary sitting on top of me, while hoots of derision emanated from the other side of the net.

"I said MINE!"

"But it was so clearly my ball, I couldn't believe you were going for it."

Gripes and mutterings rumbled on between us. One set down, and riven by internal strife, you would think our situation was hopeless. But readers, you would write off the Heath – Neary partnership at your peril. (Unless we're talking about a cricket match, in which case you'd be absolutely right to do so.) I think each of us responded inwardly to the discord between us with a steely determination to do better; a kind of 'Right, I'll show that twat who is the stronger partner here' form of motivation. Whatever the case, suddenly we clicked, whilst the Grinders suffered an equal and opposite reaction which would have thrilled Isaac Newton, going into a major slump.

In a flash, we were two sets to one up and coasting to the easy victory we always knew our abilities merited.

I'll still never know how we lost. There were many factors, all of which Neary and I analysed at great length during the bitter aftermath.

Over confidence? Might well have played a part.

Neary's sudden inability to hit groundstrokes over the net. Or volleys, or serves, or indeed any fucking shots of any description – classically executed or otherwise, for that matter? Definitely contributed to our downfall, in my view.

My failure, understandable of course, given the total collapse in my partner's play, to maintain my own game at the ridiculously high plateau of performance it had hitherto been located? Possibly, I thought, a peripheral factor.

Grant's sudden metamorphosis from gawky Scottish piece-of-wood into John McEnroe, complete with quicksilver reflexes and rapier-like volleyed winners? That certainly helped.

In the end, as we meekly surrendered the deciding set 0-6, we had to grudgingly concede that the combined name we had chosen for our team, The Heary-oes, was a poor choice, and the one the Grinders had given us, The Neaths, was more accurate.

Finally, mercifully, just when I thought I was going to drop from sleep deprivation and the over-consumption of all manner of substances which were not healthy at all, the Burchett Boys' visit was over. I bade them farewell on my way out of the door to work, having ordered a taxi to take them to the airport later in the morning in time for their midday flight.

As soon as school was over that day, I cancelled my after-school football game and trudged wearily home, already dreaming of the wonder of a sixteen-hour sleep in my bed without any foul-smelling lump thrashing about on the other side.

It was with mild surprise and, I have to admit, disappointment, therefore, that I found the three twats sitting glumly on their bags outside my flat.

Apparently, they had failed to reconfirm their return flight, and so had been bumped off it. They were absolutely livid, and I had to listen to all manner of vile condemnation of Morocco in general and Royal Air Maroc in particular, along the lines of what a tinpot airline it was, and who had ever heard of reconfirming return seats etc., etc.

I felt just a little uncomfortable, because I had indeed heard about this reconfirmation requirement. From experience of visitors to the school with whom I had spent time, I knew that all RAM return flights needed to be reconfirmed at least seventy-two hours before departure. Indeed, I had been meaning to tell the boys about it, but somehow, caught up in the hectic stromash of their visit, it had slipped my mind. I didn't see how it would really improve matters at that particular juncture if I told them I could have prevented their problem, so I judged it better to tell them later. Although, thinking back now, I'm not sure I ever did get around to doing so.

Grudgingly, I agreed to forego my much-needed sleep and accompany them back to the airport, because they had been told that there was a chance they could get on an evening flight to Frankfurt, and get a connection from there. They seemed convinced that it was somehow my fault that they had fucked up. They even asked me directly. "Haven't you ever heard about this reconfirmation crap? At the airport, they told us it was standard procedure in Morocco."

I thought it best at that point that they keep all their anger nicely focused on one target, so I answered with a diplomatically innocent, albeit not entirely accurate, "No." Nevertheless, they seemed to think, very unreasonably, that it was up to me to extricate them from the fine mess they had gotten themselves into.

As it happened, they didn't need me at all, because Alan Grant, normally the mildest of fellows, cracked. Apparently, they had already had extensive dealings with a Royal Air Maroc supervisor named Hassan in the morning, and this time Grant demanded to see him as soon as we got to the RAM desk. He then put on a magnificent virtuoso performance of obnoxity; he swore, he yelled, he manhandled, he eyeballed, he fixed people with murderous glares, he distributed glorious insults to all and sundry. He even insulted Hassan in French, to make sure he got the point, although that particular shot missed its target because he called him a *batard* which, regrettably, means a small loaf of bread.

Meanwhile, Neary and Pinder, who are both big lads, by the way, easily six feet two, stood at Grant's shoulder looking really hard.

Eventually, I felt constrained to pull Alan aside and say, 'Look, I know Moroccans. This kind of approach is never going to work. You need to grovel, be really greasy, approach things from an oblique angle... oh, and offer a bribe.'

But just as I was on the point of doing that, Hassan suddenly shouted "ALRIGHT! Okay, I'll find seats for you on this plane!"

Alan immediately subsided, and said with over-exaggerated politeness "Thank you."

Hassan whipped the tickets from Alan's grasp and stalked off, returning a couple of minutes later with three boarding passes. As he handed them over, he put his face close to Alan's and said quietly, "I'm doing this because you are very bad people, and I don't want you in my beautiful country for one minute longer. But I tell you this, I will find where you live, and if I ever visit England, I will come to your house and kill you."

The lads wanted to give me a big hug, partly in relief that they had finally escaped, and partly to thank me for a great holiday. But I brushed them off, telling them to hurry and get through passport control before the bloody plane left.

They disappeared through an automatic sliding door, and Hassan and I were left together. He turned to me, as if noticing my presence for the first time, and said menacingly, "So you live in Tangier, do you?"

"Oh no," I replied hastily. "I live in Gibraltar, or rather, in Spain. In the north. I just came over on the ferry to see those guys."

"So they are your friends?"

"Oh no, not really. I just kind of bumped into them, really. Anyway, I must be off."

I offered him my hand, but he refused to take it, and as I walked off to get a cab, I made a mental note that I had better wear a disguise every time I went to the airport from then on.

"I've been mugging old ladies all night."

Walking down the Rue Pasteur one evening, humming 'We've gotta get outta this place' to myself, I spotted a sign in the window of Gibair. Gib to London, Special Offer, One-way, only £246.

"That's the ticket," I thought.

In the office, I found that there was a seat available next Wednesday. The only thing was that although I could make the booking with them, I would have to pay for it, and pick up the ticket, from the head office in Gibraltar. I asked if they would accept payment by cheque, and they assured me that they would.

So I made my reservation then and there, and when Burnsey arrived at the weekend I persuaded him to write a cheque to Gibair, and I gave him a nice pile of dirhams in exchange.

Burnsey and I hoped to enjoy a fine final weekend together in Tangier, but there was one tricky task to complete before we could start the revels. I had been putting it off for days, but it had to be dealt with before I left.

Our first stop was The Nautilus. I hadn't been there for weeks, due to the mounting realization that my barbill had grown to such a total that there was no way I could pay it back, even if I handed over every dirham I earned between then and the end of the year. That night, I walked sheepishly up to the bar, just managing to prevent Mohamed from opening two beers for us, and told him that I needed to talk about my bill. He told me to wait a moment, and, with a mere flicker of his eyebrow, summoned Rachid himself from the table by the window where he was dining with a glamorous woman with remarkable long red hair.

I told Rachid that I was leaving Tangier for good and needed to settle up, and he asked Mohamed to total up all my chits. I waited uncomfortably while he entered sums from a terrifyingly thick wad of chits which he had extricated from my file. Before he arrived at a total, I blurted out, "Look, Rachid, I don't think there is any way I can pay all that just now, but what I propose is that I send you some cheques as soon as I start my new job in Greece. Would that be okay?"

He looked at me gravely for a few seconds, and then turned to look at the total Mohamed had just come up with.

"Can you give me anything just now?"

I had fifty dirhams in my pocket, and that was all I could offer him. I couldn't see the figure on Mohamed's pad, but it had to be well into four figures.

Rachid took my fifty, and said, "Robert, any teacher from the American School is always welcome in my restaurant. This is my home, and I don't think we should worry too much about money." Picking up the pile of chits from the counter, he went on, "I think we can find a simple solution to this little problem." And with that, he tore them all in two and dropped them in the bin.

What a wonderful man!

Burnsey, who didn't get much money in Rabat but was still much better paid than I, funded one last wild tour of the Tangerine nightspots, while I saved the bare minimum I figured I would need for my trip. Then I had a couple of days to pack all my stuff before getting the ferry over to Gibraltar.

After throwing away as much as I could, I pared my meagre possessions down to the absolute minimum and started to try to squeeze them into my backpack. When the pack was totally, thoroughly and comprehensively as full as something which has got a lot more in it than it is designed to hold, there were still a few items left. These included a grey suit which I had lugged all the way from England and worn a grand total of zero times in Morocco, a pair of rather fine walking boots which I had found in the flat when I'd moved in, and quite a large and bulky number of other things.

Some reevaluation needed to be done.

The boots were the property of the previous tenant, Ben Yarmolinski. He used to be the music teacher at our school, but he lived now in Marrakech. I'd seen him a couple of times and told him about the boots, and he had said that he would drop by and collect them some time. Sorry Ben. You had your chance.

The suit, as I said, was not exactly an essential item.

All the other stuff was not negotiable. It all had to go, but I had nothing to carry it in.

Could have been a tricky problem in many places, but in Tangier, the solution was obvious. I set off into the Petit Souk, carrying the suit and the boots, and after ten minutes of negotiating with the owner of a bag shop, I walked out of the Petit Souk carrying a fine brushed leather bag. Surprisingly enough, I still had the boots with me because, for some unaccountable reason, the bag man was not interested in them. On my way home, I came across an old bloke lying barefoot on the pavement begging. Another obvious solution jumped out at me, and I was soon carrying only the bag whilst a slightly bemused beggar was lacing up a spiffing pair of hiking boots.

Two minutes later, I bumped into Ben Yarmolinski.

"When can I come by and pick up those boots?" he asked.

"Oh, I'll be out tonight and tomorrow. Why don't you come some time next week?"

The following morning, I boarded the ferry for Gibraltar.

I was being very careful over the allocation of my dwindling supply of money at this point. Having bought my one way ferry ticket to Gibraltar, and with the cheque to pay Gibair in my pocket, I had just enough for one night in the Rock Hotel before my flight left the following morning. Food would have to wait until I got back to England where my father would surely supply some funding.

So, on arrival in Gibraltar, I walked first to the hotel and checked in, paying for the room in advance to be on the safe side. Next item of business was to pick up my flight ticket, so I trundled around the corner to the head office of that mighty international airline Gibair.

I strolled confidently up to the desk and explained that I had made a booking with their Tangier office on tomorrow's flight to London, and I would now like to collect the ticket. The nice man at the desk took out a piece of paper and ran his eyes down a list of names.

"Ah yes, Mr. Heath. That will be £246, sir. How would you like to pay?"

"By cheque."

"Certainly, sir."

I handed over the cheque. There was a pause.

"I'm sorry, sir, but I cannot accept this cheque because the name does not correspond with the name on the ticket."

This was an unforeseen snag.

The Gibair chap proved to be completely unbending on this issue. He insisted that he could not issue a ticket in the name of Mr Heath if it was to be paid for by a cheque signed by Mr Burns. He was not at all moved when I told him that nobody in the Tangier office had made any mention of such a ridiculous stipulation. Neither did he budge when I explained to him that he *had* to issue me the ticket because I had no other way of getting off Gibraltar, being without even enough funds to buy a ferry ticket back to Tangier. I asked him if he could cancel my reservation, and I could walk out of the door and then walk back in and claim to be Mr Burns and pay for a ticket in that name with the cheque. He got extremely stony-faced at that suggestion, and would not even countenance it. He wasn't at all impressed when I begged him to issue me the ticket, and bad language and threats of violence (the Alan Grant technique) met with an equal lack of success.

The only way he was going to give me that ticket was if I paid him £246 in cash. I had five pounds in my pocket, which left a bit of a shortfall, even according to the most optimistic of calculations. The only thing the bastard would say was that he would hold the seat for me right up until 8.30 a.m. the following morning, which was half an hour after the office opened.

So there I was in a bit of a bind. A conundrum. How to get hold of £246 on a stupid lump of anachronistic colonial rock where I knew nobody and credit cards hadn't even been properly invented yet.

Gibraltar has bookies where you can bet on British horse races. All I had to do was pick a winner with odds of 50 to 1, and put my fiver on it. Forget that!

But wait a minute... I DID know somebody! The head of PE at St Joseph's School. He had hosted us for the basketball tournament the previous year, and... searching frantically through my address book, I found that I did indeed have a phone number for him. He had been a nice guy, and we had been out for a couple of drinks together.

He was a nice guy, but was he a nice enough guy that he would give me, someone he barely knew and who admitted he was leaving Gibraltar the very next day probably never to return, £246?

Did I even have the gall to ask him? Well that wasn't an issue because he was my only hope.

I rang his number. He was in, which was good. And he remembered who I was, which was better. And he sounded pleased to hear from me, which was better still. And then I said, "I've got a huge favour to ask you."

"Go ahead, what is it?" the fool replied.

"Well..." and I gave him what was probably a wild and garbled explanation of my predicament. "So if there's any way you can get hold of £246 this evening, can you lend it to me, and as soon as I get to England I will have my father send you a cheque."

Would YOU have given an almost total stranger 250 quid against a promise of a cheque in the mail from his dad? Luckily for me, this guy was either mad enough or generous enough to agree to the idea. He arranged to meet me in the middle of town, and armed with his cash card (which HAD been invented) we paid a visit to the Bank of Gibraltar. There was one wobbly moment when he said that his card often failed to register, but this time it worked a treat and I had the money. After profuse and grovelling thanks, I retired to the hotel where I spent the whole night sitting still so that nothing else could go wrong.

When the Gibair office opened at eight the next morning, I was waiting outside, and I marched straight up to the desk where Mr Stickler was on duty again.

"I would like to pay for a reserved ticket on this morning's flight to London, please."

Gitface obviously thought I was going to try to pass off Burnsey's cheque again, so he smarmily asked me, "How are you going to pay?"

"In cash!" I replied, producing a wad of notes from my pocket and slamming it onto the counter.

Now he was suddenly Mr Allsmiles. "Oh, you got the money then. That's good… How did you do it?"

"I've been mugging old ladies all night. Now can I have my ticket, please."

He glanced up into my face, not sure for a moment if I was serious. I was not in the best of humours, and when he saw my scowl, he really didn't know whether to believe me or not. He filled out my ticket as quickly as he could, his hand trembling ever-so slightly, and I took it from him and left without another word.

At the airport, I joined the queue to check in for the London flight. At last, I was going to get away from this weird little corner of the globe. It had certainly been a funny old time. I had met all kinds of larger-than-life characters: murderers, villains, rakes (I think – I never really knew exactly what the exact definition of a rake was, but I was pretty sure that whatever it was, some of the people I met in Tangier must have matched it), millionaires and beggars, people from dozens of countries. I had been threatened with knives, propositioned by homosexuals, and caught up in riots. I had eaten some wonderful food, consumed prodigious amounts of alcohol, and experienced the extraordinary highs and lows of the hashish fiend.

Dull, it had not been, but by the end of two years, I had had enough. I had the offer of a new job in

Thessaloniki, and all I craved by that point was a normal humdrum existence. I'd had enough of all the drama.

So I felt an intense wave of relief flood over me when I got to the front of the queue and handed over my ticket.

"Thank you. And your passport, please?"

Aaaaarrgghh! My passport!

I stood there, desperately patting all my pockets hoping to find a passport-shaped lump, but it was useless because I remembered at that instant that I had left my passport at the Rock Hotel. I had handed it over when I had checked in, and when I left that morning, I had been so distracted thinking about whether I would get my ticket or not, I had forgotten to collect it.

I tore out of the terminal and leaped into the first cab on the rank. I had one Gibraltar pound note left in my possession. "Can you get me to the Rock Hotel and back here in twenty minutes for this?" I yelled, maniacally waving the note at the driver. It didn't actually constitute the greatest incentive a cabbie has been offered, but this guy must have seen I was desperate, or maybe he watched a lot of movies. Either way, he agreed, and we set off at a screech.

Of course, the Rock Hotel chose to be at the diametrically opposite end of Gibraltar to the airport, but luckily, the traffic was light. Soon enough, he pulled up outside the hotel, and I leaped from the vehicle and raced up to the door. As I rushed through, I bumped smack into someone who was rushing out. We barged into each other, chest-to-chest, and bounced back, giving each other a startled look. Astonishingly, it was the desk clerk, and he was holding my passport in his hand. I never knew what he was doing with it, but I later surmised that he must have just discovered that they still had my passport and, knowing which flight I was on, had been trying to race it to the airport. I didn't have time to ask him; after a stunned moment when we both looked at each other, I grabbed the passport from him, yelled, "Thanks!" over my shoulder, and scrambled back into the taxi.

All that remained was a nerve-racking drive back through the quaint and infuriatingly narrow and convoluted streets of the city, profuse but hurried thanks to Robert de Niro, a mad rush back to the Gibair desk, and before long I was watching the wing of the plane dip towards the glittering blue water as we banked to climb up, all the way around the rock of Gibraltar. The nose of the plane pointed steadfastly north, and Tangier and Morocco fell away behind us.

The Tangerine Dream was over.